We know what kind of Indian we are. . . .

We look at each other. Four reservation kids. We know what kind of Indian we are. The kind of Indian you don't see in Hollywood movies. No noble savages. No horses or headdresses. No tipis and no buffalo. No Tonto (which means "idiot" in Spanish) to the Lone Ranger. We are a different kind. The kind of Indian who gets ignored at best and treated like dirt at worst. The kind of Indian who lives in secondhand trailers or in old houses with no insulation. The kind of Indian who ends up in foster homes or whose parents fall off the wagon and get killed in car accidents or just disappear. The kind of Indian who knows that hope rhymes with nope.

"Bruchac perfectly captures a boy's pride in his culture and the pain and anger he feels when his rich identity is mocked by a 'tomahawk chop' from a sports fan. Readers who see injustice in their own lives will admire how much Chris accomplishes with a simple message of respect."
—*Booklist*

Joseph Bruchac is the author of more than fifty acclaimed books for children and adults, many of which draw upon the Native American culture that is part of his heritage. He has won several awards for the body of his work, including the New York Library Association's Knickerbocker Award for Juvenile Literature.

Joseph Bruchac lives in Greenfield Center, New York.

OTHER PUFFIN BOOKS YOU MAY ENJOY

The heart of a chief
must beat with
the hearts of the people

The heart of a chief
is the beat of the drum

The beat of the drum
is the heartbeat
of our land.

J.B.

THE
HEART
OF
A CHIEF

JOSEPH BRUCHAC

PUFFIN BOOKS

To the memory of Mdawelasis
and Nanapashamet
and
To all the Children of the Dawn
J.B.

PUFFIN BOOKS
Published by the Penguin Group
Penguin Putnam Books for Young Readers,
345 Hudson Street, New York, New York 10014, U.S.A.
Penguin Books Ltd, 27 Wrights Lane, London W8 5TZ, England
Penguin Books Australia Ltd, Ringwood, Victoria, Australia
Penguin Books Canada Ltd, 10 Alcorn Avenue, Toronto, Ontario, Canada M4V 3B2
Penguin Books (N.Z.) Ltd, 182-190 Wairau Road, Auckland 10, New Zealand

Penguin Books Ltd, Registered Offices: Harmondsworth, Middlesex, England

First published in the United States of America by Dial Books for Young Readers,
a member of Penguin Putnam Inc., 1998
Published by Puffin Books,
a division of Penguin Putnam Books for Young Readers, 2001

15 17 19 20 18 16 14

THE LIBRARY OF CONGRESS HAS CATALOGED THE DIAL EDITION AS FOLLOWS:
Bruchac, Joseph, date.
The heart of a chief: a novel / by Joseph Bruchac.—1st ed
p. cm.
Summary: An eleven-year-old Penacook Indian boy living on a reservation faces his
father's alcoholism, a controversy surrounding plans for a casino on a tribal island,
and insensitivity toward Native Americans in his school and nearby town.
ISBN 0-8037-2276-1
[1. Indian reservations—Fiction. 2. Penacook Indians—Fiction. 3. Indians of North
America—New Hampshire—Fiction. 4. Alcoholism—Fiction.] I. Title.
PZ7.B82816He 1998 [Fic]—dc21 97-49248 CIP AC

Puffin Books ISBN 0-14-131236-X

Printed in the United States of America

Author's Note

The Heart of a Chief is a novel, but it is based on the realities of contemporary Indian America, and on the many years I've spent working with Indian kids in schools throughout America. On reservations such as Akwesasne Mohawk on the St. Lawrence River; Odanak in Canada; the Onondaga Indian Reservation in central New York; the Mohegan Nation of Connecticut; and the Passamaquoddy Reservation near Pleasant Point, Maine, I've met young people like my story's hero, Chris. I often do workshops in which I encourage Native American children to write their own poems and tell their own stories. I've learned a great deal from them about courage, toughness, and faith in the face of overwhelming odds. Whatever is true in the book, I owe to them.

I decided, however, not to set this novel on a real reservation. Some of the issues in the book, such as casino gambling, leadership, and alcohol abuse, are too sensitive for me to do that. Instead, I have imagined a reservation where none currently exist, although they should: in New Hampshire. The Penacook are one of the nations of my own Western Abenaki people; but there is, at present, no state or federally recognized Penacook community.

SEEING THE ISLAND

It's hard to see it through the mist, but it's right out there across the bay. The island. Where I'm sitting, you can get a good view of it when the clouds clear away. Or, as Doda would say, when the fog walks back across the wide lake to sleep in the marshy lands near the sunset.

This is a good place to sit. I'm comfortable now, even though rain is falling and I'm all wet. But I was already wet before I came to sit here. This rock was shaped long ago to make a seat big enough for two people: one to tell the story and one to listen. It wasn't made by a person, at least not in the way you'd understand that word, person, in English. But it was shaped by someone, a very ancient someone called Gluskabe by my people, as a place to rest and listen and look out at the island. So I'm going to sit here in Gluskabe's Seat and tell you this story.

Out there a seagull skitters just above the water. Its wings flash and then it's gone into the clouds that fly with wings as white as the gull's. Even though I can't see the gull anymore, I can hear it speak its name in our old language: *ka-ahhk!* And if you listen close, you can hear the crows who are flying up over us. Flying toward the island, where they have their nests in the cedars that are taller than any of the trees here on the mainland. *Gah-gah,* they say, announcing themselves. I can hear seven of them.

In the old days we could recognize everything around us because everything spoke its own name to us. I can't speak our language the way Doda, my grandfather, can, but he tells me that I just have to keep listening. I'm learning. He helps me some, but mostly I have to listen. The land keeps the language. The island keeps it real good, Doda says.

It's pretty hard for him to walk now. Can't hunt no moose on snowshoe no more, he says, and then laughs a little laugh that is soft like a feather touching your face. But when I can help him get down to the boat—he has to crawl into it while I hold his crutches—he does just fine rowing. Better than me. I'm kind of small for my age. When his brown hands wrap around the oars, his fingers are as thick and strong as cedar roots.

We like to row together out to the island, to the little beach that is around on the sunset side. It has white sand and small, perfectly round stones that are smooth as glass when you cup them in your palm. Then he describes everything to me in the old language. Lets everything show itself by speaking its name.

Things aren't always so clear in English. Don't get me wrong—I've got nothing against English. Auntie says it is our language too, and don't let no one tell you it isn't. In our family we've been speaking it for about four hundred years, when we weren't speaking our old language or using French. Four centuries is a long time for a person, but not long at all for a rock like the one I'm sitting on—or an island. So I'm telling this story in English, mostly.

In English my name means two saints. Well, actually, one ex-saint and one saint who is sort of shaky. My last name is the shaky saint's: Nicola. That's the way we say Nicholas in our language. Like Saint Nicholas. Back when the Europeans gave us names, we still said and spelled them our own way a lot of times. Saint Paul became Sabael. Saint Baptiste became Sabattis. And Nicholas became Nicola—my last name.

My first name is Chris, short for Christopher. And I have a Mr. Christopher medal, as Mito calls it. It used to be a Saint Christopher medal when Mito was my age, but then the Catholic Church demoted Saint Christopher because they think he never really lived. He'd been the patron saint of travelers. Mito says traveling must have got a lot more dangerous back when Mr. Christopher lost his halo. Mito is my dad. He's funny when he hasn't been drinking.

I have another name. Doda is the one who mostly uses it. But I won't say it to you in our language. It's really only supposed to be spoken when you're on the water, or in sight of it. But it is okay, Doda says, to tell what it means in English. It means something like Log Resting Firm on Both Shores and Wide Enough to Walk Upon. Bridge is probably the closest word in English.

Now here's the story. Like Doda says, this story was out walking around, and when it saw me sitting here it decided to come over and stay for a while. Listen to what it has to say.

1 Morning Songs

The radio beside my bed buzzes and then begins to talk to me in Penacook. But it doesn't speak Penacook for long. Muskrat Mike, the morning DJ on KOOK, only knows a few words. He's pretty cool and knows a lot about music, but he isn't young enough to have gone to the Penacook Indian School.

The kids at the school take an extra enrichment class in Penacook. Elders like Doda go in once a day to talk Indian with them, and by the time they get to third grade some of them can speak it okay. I went there through third grade, and Celeste still goes there. She's seven. But now I get bused to school off the reservation. I'm eleven by how the school reckons it. Ten winters, Doda would say. You haven't really lived a year until you've lived through another winter. I'm starting sixth grade at Rangerville Junior High, and today is the first day of school. Lucky me.

"*Kwey, nidobak!* Hey, buddies! Wake it and shake it out there," Muskrat Mike says. "We're kicking off the broadcast day with the title cut from the new

Bill Miller CD. Then for you young bears taking that long trek on the yellow beast, keep your headphones on. 'Cause Kurt Cobain knew what it's like to be going away from home."

Muskrat Mike's voice crackles now and then as he talks. Headphones or not, there's no chance any of us on the bus to the schools in Rangerville will hear much of his show once we go past St. Anne's Church and around the hill past the sign. It reads Welcome to Penacook Reservation on the front in letters made to look like birch bark logs. (On the back someone has sprayed START BREATHING AGAIN.) The sign marks the effective range of KOOK Radio. Two miles in any direction, almost the exact boundaries of our little reservation. The joke is that whenever KOOK goes off the air, and it happens pretty often, it is because they can't afford to buy a new flashlight battery.

I sit up and take a deep breath. Bill Miller, who is a Stockbridge Indian, is playing flute on the radio. The reception on the radio is as clear as a cloudless sky. It blends in fine with the smell of sweetgrass and wood smoke and food cooking. No place in the world smells as good as the little one-story house that Doda and Auntie have lived in since the world was new.

I couldn't take a bath last night because the tub is full of sweetgrass that Auntie is soaking. She'll be braiding it all day today and weaving it into her baskets. Sweetgrass is supposed to bring good health.

Even though her fingers are stiff from arthritis, it sure has brought good health to Auntie. She's out-lived three husbands and all of her brothers and sisters except for Doda. She doesn't think she is old, though.

"I'm young," she says. "Nobody ever gets real old these days. Now back then our people really got old. Back before they started eating this French food. Then they would live a hundred fifty years. That is old."

French food is anything from bacon and eggs to a Big Mac. Anything that isn't the kind of food our people ate before the Europeans came. I asked her once, when I was little and Mito and Mom had brought me and Celeste to visit her and Doda, what we Pena-cooks ate back then.

She started talking in Penacook and didn't stop for almost an hour. I remember the way my dad turned to my mom and winked.

"And that was just for appetizers," Mito said.

Mom had laughed. When she laughed, it was like the sound of wind chimes.

"Auntie," she said, "what about frybread?"

Auntie had not answered her. But Doda did.

"Frybread," he said, "is the Indian national anthem."

I look over at Doda's bed, which is next to mine. The little house only has four rooms. Doda and I sleep together in the room on the north side. Auntie and

Celeste have their beds in the south room. The house is built the way a wigwam would have been built back then. Its outside doors and windows all face the dawn. Its two inside doors lead from the bedrooms into the combination kitchen and living room. The bathroom is at the back of that room. Some houses on the reservation still have outhouses, but my grandfather and great-aunt have indoor plumbing. Electricity too. Auntie's stove, though, is a woodstove with an oven in it. She and Doda call it the new stove. It is clean and shiny, but I looked once at the back of it where the name Kalamazoo and a date is stamped—1914.

Doda's bed is empty. He always gets up to greet the sun. Some days he wakes me up to help him. Those days we make a little fire up on the hill outside. I am very good at gathering just the right kind of sticks for the fire. Doda carefully takes his dark brown deerskin pouch out of the deep back pocket of his overalls. His lips move to speak words I never hear from anyone else as he unwinds the rawhide string to open the pouch. I hold his crutches while he places some tobacco on the coals as the sun comes up. Then he sings a song to greet the sun. He says that song is so old that the sun taught the people to sing it. I know it and I sing it in my head with Doda.

I lean over and put a hand on Doda's bed. His bed is perfectly made. The corners are tucked in and the blanket pulled so tight that if you dropped a penny on it, the penny would bounce. Doda learned that from his time in the United States Army.

Just about every Penacook man is a decorated veteran. When they have the Veterans Day Parade in Rangerville, the Penacook veterans almost out-number all the others. The decorated veterans all wear their medals, but the Penacook decorated vet-erans look like Christmas trees because they have so many. The medals just glitter in the sunlight and the men hold their heads up so proud. It is something to see. Doda's war, if you can believe it, was World War II. He fought the Germans. And the Italians too, if I remember right.

I get dressed in the clean clothes Auntie has laid out on my wooden chair. I never hear her come in, but she does that every day. I make my bed twice, trying to get it like Doda's. Good and tight. I have a quarter in my pocket. I hold it up shoulder height and let it fall on the blanket. Plop. No bounce. Maybe it is too heavy.

Rap-rap, rap-rap-rap. Five knocks on my door. That is Celeste. Our breakfast is ready. I reach over and rap back twice. I'll be right there.

Then I walk over to my wall calendar. I take the black pen and draw a diagonal line down across today's date. If I survive to make it home alive, I'll draw the other diagonal tonight to make it an X. Then it'll be one day of school down and only two hundred million more to go.

2 Round One

When you get off the bus, you are on your own. But I still try to blend into the crowd. It's a little easier to do that on the first day of school, especially if you're just starting junior high. I think I can recognize the other sixth graders because we are the ones trying not to be noticed. The older kids are the confident ones. They're yelling at each other. A couple of wide-shouldered guys are tossing a football back and forth.

My friend Pizza nudges me.

"The big one there," he says, his voice sort of wistful, "that's Thumper Wheelock. He gave somebody who tried to block him a concussion last year."

I've heard of Thumper Wheelock. But before I can say so, two girls—both of them taller than me—walk between us as if we weren't there. They are talking about cheerleading. One of them does a spontaneous cartwheel for her friend. Right in my direction. I get out of her way fast. That separates me from Pizza and the other Penacook kids who were on the bus with me.

A bell starts ringing from the top of the redbrick school building, which looks just like the front of this maximum security prison I saw in a movie. I'm starting to panic. I'm caught in a wave of kids moving toward the front door of the school. A riptide. I don't think my feet are touching the pavement anymore. It reminds me of something I read about a place in Australia with these tides that pull you under and back out to sea, where great white sharks are waiting to eat you. The tide sweeps me up the stairs and through the mouth of the door. A doorway gaping wide like big jaws. I brace myself for the first set of teeth chomping down on me.

I feel the ache in my stomach that comes when I am getting upset. It's psychosomatic. I read that word two days ago in my dictionary. That's what you call bodily symptoms resulting from mental conflict. But knowing the word doesn't make the stomachache go away. It feels like a fist has been punched into my gut.

I know how it feels to get hit in the stomach, but just in case I don't, I am about to get a refresher course in it as I try to work my way through the crowd. I'm starting to catch up to some of the other Penacook kids, whose backs are just barely visible in the hallway ahead of me. They're sticking together, the way little fish do, swimming fast in a big bunch for safety. If I can reach the others, I'm thinking, the sharks won't get me.

My friends are ten steps ahead of me and the crowd

※ 11

of kids is thinning out as they enter the various rooms. I think I can catch up. Mistake. I stumble— or maybe someone trips me. I take a step trying to keep my balance, flailing my arms and bumping hard into someone short who is just starting to pass in front of me. My hands knock something out of that person's arms. It whops down onto the floor. I almost step on it, but a shoulder slams into me, knocking me back as a small but unpleasantly hard elbow is jabbed right into the middle of my stomach. I double over.

"Jerk," says a tearful voice.

It is a girl's voice. She is the short person who bodyblocked and elbowed me out of the way to protect whatever it was that I knocked out of her grasp. She is already picking it up: a diorama on an eighteen-inch-wide piece of plywood. There is a neat little wigwam in the center made out of bent sticks and birch bark. Somehow, even though I am having a hard time breathing, I notice that the wigwam looks real. She also hasn't glued any of those dumb plastic *Indian in the Cupboard* figures next to it.

Making a noise like a ruptured pelican, I turn my head to look at the girl's face. I've never seen her before. Long dark hair and bangs, blue eyes, a nose that is a little crooked, but I like its shape. She's not smiling now, but I think that she must look really nice when she smiles. She is straightening out the wigwam, which got knocked a little crooked. But her diorama doesn't seem to be messed up much. I'm glad about that. I want to apologize, but I am still struggling for breath and I can't say anything more intelligent than "Ah-awwkk, eeehhk." Pelicanese for "excuse me."

But she doesn't speak the language. She turns away from me and then goes through a door on the left of the hall. I'm the only kid left standing there as the bell rings again.

I shake my head and I have to smile. I have been beat up by a girl and it isn't even nine o'clock yet. End of round one. But it isn't over yet because the door that girl has disappeared through is Room 6A. My new homeroom.

No matter how bad things seem, remember one thing. They can always get worse. In Rangerville Junior High that is probably going to be my maxim. I feel like an exposed nerve ending. If I were a rabbit I would start sniffing the air. If I were a deer I would be swiveling my ears back and forth to listen for predators sneaking up behind me.

I know that's not the way I'm supposed to be. Doda explained it to me when I was having one of my nervous times. He stood me in front of the bathroom mirror with white scrolled ferns all around the edge of it. That mirror is so old that looking into it is like looking into a cloud. In your reflection you are surrounded by mist.

"Look where your eyes are," he said. "When deer and rabbit were made, they were made with eyes on the sides of their heads. That way they see things sneaking up on them from all sides. They were made to be hunted. But wolf, lynx, mountain lion, they were made with eyes in front. They are made to be hunters."

Doda paused then. He just thought the question, he didn't say it. And I answered.

"My eyes are in front, Doda."

Eyes ahead, I go into the classroom and quickly slide into the wrong seat—too close to the front. Big mistake. It's an unwritten rule that Indian kids who don't want to get in trouble sit in the back. All the Indian kids, from us lowly sixth graders on up to the three Penacooks who are in high school, know that. For some reason the teacher isn't in the room yet. A redheaded kid is leaning over another desk nearby, talking with a friend. He turns, stares at me, and then makes a motion with his thumb. I'm in his seat. I clear out fast, scooting like a rabbit seeking cover. As I slide into the one empty desk left near the back, I bang my knee so hard that it makes a sound everyone in the room can hear. Kids laugh. I put my head down so that I can't see the faces of the people who are laughing and I bite my lip to keep from groaning from the pain.

The girl who elbowed me turns out to be Katie. I learn that during roll call, when the teacher, Mr. Dougal, calls it off and she says, "Here!" I write "Katie" down on the inside back cover of my notebook and watch her out of the corner of my eye. Her long black hair falls over the side of her face like a curtain between the two of us.

Bad luck comes in threes. I've heard that saying a lot and proved it more than once. Three is a magic number for white people. You know, all those stories with three wishes. Three strikes and you're out. Lots of things in European culture come in threes. I am hoping this morning that whatever my third piece of bad luck is going to be won't be fatal. I am also hoping that this bad luck isn't an Indian thing. Indian things—like the seasons and the directions—come in fours.

It turns out I'm so busy trying to avoid getting into trouble that I walk right into it. Schools are full of rules. There are the written rules that everyone knows—adults and kids alike. Rules like no throwing things in the classroom, no yelling or running in the halls.

Then there are the unwritten rules. Usually, only the kids know them. There are no meetings where someone gets up and spells them out. From the first day we just seem to pick them up by some kind of adolescent radar—invisible signals in the air that only a kid's antenna can receive. Or maybe we know those rules by instinct, the way salmon know they are supposed to swim upstream. Rules like what clothes you have to wear to be accepted into the right crowd, or not looking a certain way at the wrong people.

As I limp around the corner on my way to gym class, making sure I don't make eye contact with anyone or bump into anybody, I make my mistake. I've taken a wrong turn. I'm heading for the eighth-grade classrooms. I see a group of eighth graders heading down the hall in my direction, talking and laughing. Avoid them, my radar says. But how? I panic, push open the door at my back, and slip inside.

My footsteps echo on the tile in the empty room. I am in the larger of the two boys' rooms on the first floor. My skin turns cold. I have broken one of those unwritten rules. A big one. This boys' room is for seventh- and eighth-grade boys only. Not for worms, which is what *all* sixth graders are to the kids in the upper classes. The rumor is that the older boys do drug deals in here.

Right now, though, the room seems empty. Maybe I am not about to be killed. I can hide in one of the stalls until the bell rings and then sneak out when no one's around. I'll be late to gym class, but detention is better than being disemboweled. Then I notice that the door to the stall on the end is closed. A toilet flushes. I freeze like a deer in headlights. The door opens. And the kid who comes out—the kid who sees me standing there unable to move or breathe—is Thumper Wheelock. The biggest kid in eighth grade. The same one Pizza pointed out to me. Offensive tackle on the modified football team. Big enough to already be the heavyweight on the high school JV wrestling squad. According to what everyone says, he got his nickname because he thumped a couple of guys from the next town over who tried to push him around at the county fair once. Maybe it was three guys he beat up. Sent them to the hospital. Which was where I would soon be going.

Thumper Wheelock finishes buckling his belt and then takes a step toward me. I hear the deep-voiced narrator from one of those nature shows: *"Its prey in sight, the giant bear slowly begins to move in for the kill."* Somebody is giggling in a high-pitched voice. I wish that person would shut up. Then I realize the person giggling is me. Three strikes and I'm out.

Thumper Wheelock reaches out his big grizzly-bear paw toward me. It motions for me to move aside.

"Excuse me," he says, "I wanta use the sink."

I step aside, trying not to watch as he washes his hands.

"You still here?"

I can't find my voice, so I just nod to his reflection in the mirror.

"In the wrong bathroom, aren't you?" he says.

His voice is so calm that I am able to answer him in something other than a Mickey Mouse squeak.

"Unh-hunh," I say.

He turns around, shaking the water from his hands.

"It's a dumb rule," he says. "No reason you younger kids shouldn't be able to use this bathroom. It's those burnouts who got nothing better to do than pick on the little guys who make dumb rules like that. You don't have cooties, do you?"

He smiles at me and I realize that he is actually teasing me in a friendly way.

"Not the last time I looked," I say.

Thumper laughs. He finishes wiping his hands thoroughly on a paper towel, rolls it into a neat ball, and hookshots it into the trash barrel. The bell rings. "Gotta get to my next class. See ya around."

He goes out the door. As it swings shut, I realize that this has not been my number three bad luck experience after all. I smile as I walk out of the downstairs boys' bathroom and watch Thumper's broad back disappear down the hall.

And when I get to gym class, no one notices that I am late. The gym teacher is an easygoing guy, Asian American, I think. Even though I'm not the biggest kid, I've always liked gym class. I've got good balance and I'm used to running distances. After the first lap around the gym, my knee actually stops hurting. We run through calisthenics and push-ups and sit-ups and I do okay.

Katie is in my Language Arts class. As it begins, I look toward her again. She is sitting three seats over and two rows closer to the front than me. But Katie still won't look my way, though I don't really know why it is that I want to make eye contact with her.

I realize that something good has been happening as this day goes on. I think my eyes have been gradually moving from the side of my head to where they belong, in the front. If I look at myself in Doda's mirror, I won't have to turn my head from side to side.

I picture myself looking in that mirror again, but this time I don't just see my own face. I also see the faces of Doda and Auntie behind me, and in the misty cloud of the mirror I see more faces than I can count. They look familiar, even though I don't know who they are. I don't know their names. But I know they are Penacooks. They are all around me and they are behind me and they are with me.

I raise my hand. Mr. Dougal, my homeroom teacher, is also my teacher for Language Arts. He has just turned away from the board to look at something on his desk. He is surprised to see my hand up, but he points at me with the chalk.

"Mr. Nicola?"

"Can I move closer to the front?" I ask. "I'm having a hard time seeing the board from here."

Mr. Dougal raises one eyebrow. "There are no assigned seats in here, Mr. Nicola. Be my guest."

As I move up to the front row, I notice that Katie is looking my way. I glance over and catch her eye. Her lips are parted as if she is about to mouth silent words. Then she closes her mouth, looks down, and the wall of black hair comes between us again.

The class goes on. We are going to be discussing *The Sign of the Beaver.* Mr. Dougal talks about it while kids pretend they are not falling asleep. He loves the book. Like a lot of teachers in Rangerville, it seems he admires Indians in the past and doesn't really pay much attention to those of us who are still here. Or maybe he thinks that this book should make us feel proud we are Indian. But I have already read *The Sign of the Beaver,* which is about my people.

I am still seeing that mirror with all my ancestors' faces in it when I raise my hand again. I have to say something.

"Mr. Nicola?" This time both of his eyebrows are raised. He looks down at me over his hooked nose. It makes him look like a bird of prey.

"There's something wrong," I say.

"Wrong?"

"About the book."

"I have been assured that it is an accurate portrayal of the times. It's a balanced view of both the settlers and the Native Americans, wouldn't you agree?"

That is supposed to end the discussion. "Wouldn't you agree?" means that a teacher knows more than you do and it is time to shut up. But I don't.

"No," I say.

Everyone in class is awake now. I can feel their eyes on my back from where I sit.

"Then what is your point of disagreement?" Mr. Dougal is leaning on his desk now, a hawk about to dive down on a rabbit. But I am not a rabbit.

"The end of the book," I say. "At the end the Indians just go away. But that isn't what happened." I look back around the classroom before I turn back to Mr. Dougal. "We didn't go away. They tried to drive us off the land. They put bounties on our scalps. They burned our villages. But we didn't go away."

Mr. Dougal has his hand on his chin now as he looks at me. I can't tell what his look means, but it doesn't shut me up.

"*Nda,*" I say in Penacook. "No. We did not go away. We're still here."

There is a long silence in the classroom. Maybe

I'm in trouble now. I sit there, feeling glad that my friend Gartersnake is not in this class with me. Gartersnake has been reading about the American Indian Movement lately and he's been trying a little too hard to be a real Indian. He even talked about giving himself a Mohawk haircut until I pointed out that Mohawks and Penacooks were enemies. He finally settled on dark sunglasses like the ones John Trudell, the Lakota guy who was one of the founders of AIM and is now a rock star, wears. If Gartersnake were here, I know I would be in big trouble because he would have pumped his fist in the air after my little speech and said "Right on, Red Brother." Instead, there is this ominous silence.

But the silence gives Mr. Dougal a chance to collect himself. I think of how my dad would have given him credit for that. Mito has said to me more than once that one thing he learned about the world outside the reservation is that most people in it don't give themselves a chance to think things over before they act. Mr. Dougal, though, is thinking. Then he nods.

"Actually," he says, "that is a good point. I'd like to talk with you more about that sometime, Mr. Nicola. Ah, in English."

He laughs and the class laughs with him. But I know they aren't laughing at me. It is like sharing a joke we all made together. I'm still feeling wary, but not like a rabbit or a deer. More like a wolf sniffing the wind.

Mr. Dougal is already going on to something else.

Tomorrow's reading assignment, the standardized testing we'll be doing. Some of the kids in the class are listening. Some are drawing pictures while they pretend to take notes. Others are going back to sleep with their eyes open. And then the bell rings.

As I stand up and head for the door, I find myself next to Katie. I squeeze back so that she has plenty of elbow room to go by me. I don't want to take a chance on bumping into her again. But I'm close enough to say something that only she will hear.

"I'm really sorry I wrecked your diorama."

She throws her head so that her hair goes back over her shoulder. It makes me think of the way a horse tosses its mane. She looks straight at me and she is sort of smiling.

"It's just that I worked on it all summer. I wanted to get off to a really good start this year. But it wasn't wrecked," she says. She reaches into her bag and pulls out a little white bottle. "Elmer's glue, see? I was prepared."

"I wasn't," I say, pointing at my stomach where she elbowed me. "You bodyblock like a forward on a hockey team!"

"I'm such a hothead," Katie says. She puts her head down and mumbles something. We're in the hall now and about to go in different directions.

"What?" I say. I have this impulse to reach out and brush her long hair away so that I can see her face again.

She doesn't turn back to me, but she repeats what she said loudly enough so that I can hear it.

"My mom always blames it on my Indian blood. I'm Indian too."

And then she is running down the hall so fast that I hope no teacher sees her, because she will get in trouble for sure.

Heading home on our bus, I tell Belly Button about what happened in Language Arts and what Katie said. Belly Button is my best friend. He's the most sensible one of us Penacook kids and so I figure that he will understand—or, even better, help me understand. By now I am really confused. I don't know if I've just had a great day or a terrible one. But Belly Button only makes it more confusing. He ignores what I had said in class and goes straight to the heart of what I am really confused about.

"She said she was Indian?"

"Unh-hunh."

"Anybody can say they're Indian. What kind of Indian?"

Gartersnake, who is listening to it all, turns around in his seat, lifts up his shades, and joins in.

"Yeah," Gartersnake says, "what kind? Hollywood? Calcutta?"

Pizza leans over from the seat next to us. Of course he's been listening too. "Cherokee Princess?" he asks.

We look at each other. Four reservation kids. We know what kind of Indian we are. The kind of Indian you don't see in Hollywood movies. No noble savages. No horses or headdresses. No tipis and no buffalo. No Tonto (which means "idiot" in Spanish) to the Lone Ranger. We are a different kind. The kind of Indian who gets ignored at best and treated like dirt at worst. The kind of Indian who lives in second-hand trailers or in old houses with no insulation. The kind of Indian who ends up in foster homes or whose parents fall off the wagon and get killed in car accidents or just disappear. The kind of Indian who knows that hope rhymes with nope.

Katie doesn't seem like us. But she'd been carrying that diorama with a wigwam on it. And she'd said that her mother blamed her hot temper on her Indian blood.

I nod. My friends are right.

"Cherokee Princess," I answer. I lift up my hand and Pizza gives me a high five. We all laugh, but I hate myself for calling Katie a Cherokee Princess, especially because it's probably true.

Mito explained it to me when I was old enough to understand. We were sitting by the lake skipping stones across the water.

"Wherever you go," he said, "you are always going to meet people who will say something like, 'Hey, you're an Indian? My great-great-grandmother was an Indian. She was a real Cherokee Princess.'"

Mito laughed then, that laugh of his which didn't mean he was really amused. He sidearmed a stone and it skipped eight times before it sank.

"Cherokee Princess," he said. "It's always got to be royalty of some kind. They don't know that we never had kings or queens or princes and princesses before the white people came. Our people weren't like that, and neither were the Cherokees. Our leaders always spoke for the people. They never told the people what to do."

He hefted another stone and heaved it. This one skipped a dozen times, leaving circles that spread into each other on the calm face of the listening water.

"And why has it always got to be Cherokee? Don't they know there were about a thousand different tribes? I know there's a lot of people who got Indian blood, but they can't all be Cherokees. Unless those so-called Cherokee princesses all had about two hundred kids each after they married some white guy."

Mito bent down and handed me a round, flat rock. I tried to throw it just the way he did. But I only got four skips out of it. It was okay, though. I knew that my father knew I was trying. And he knew I was listening to him and I'd remember what he said.

He walked up the slope away from the road and I followed him. Finally he and I sat down on the flat rock shaped by Gluskabe, helper to the Great Spirit.

"Another thing," Mito said, his hands rubbing the smooth stone of Gluskabe's Seat, "that is strange about this whole Cherokee thing. It is never a Cherokee Prince. It's always got to be a woman. Even now, generations later, they can't accept the fact that way back then, one of their great-great-grandmothers might have married an Indian man."

"A real live Cherokee Princess," I say again to my friends. They nod their heads, as if that finishes it. But I know that it doesn't. Dumb as it is, I am going to ask Katie. Not tomorrow, but maybe the next day or next week.

What kind of Indian?

3 The Little Guys

It is Saturday morning and I have survived the entire first week of school. That's a big plus one. But on Monday I will be back in the shark tank. Equally big minus one. Except the weekend is only two days and the week is five. Maybe that is actually minus five. I'm already buried in negative numbers and I haven't even gotten around to thinking about the big things. Mom's death. Dad's drinking. Doda and Auntie both being so old that they might die in their sleep any night now, and then what would happen to Celeste and me? What would happen to our island if no one like Doda and Auntie was still around to stop them?

I am getting hysterical. My eyes are not yet open, but my fists are clenched. If I didn't chew my fingernails short, they would be cutting into my palms. My heart is beating so fast that it sounds like a drum solo.

But the little voice that is singing from somewhere is slow. Slow and gentle. Soft, but louder than the drum solo. I listen to it. And the drum solo that is my crazed heartbeat slows down to match the rhythm of that song.

It is Auntie's voice coming from the other room, where she is bent over her kitchen table stirring something in a bowl. Even with my eyes closed, I can see her. Long gray braids swaying as she stirs. I can hear the tap of her spoon against the side of the big wooden bowl. Tapping along in time with the music. Her singing is so sweet that it calms my heart down. It stops the counting that was flapping back and forth inside my head like a trapped bird's wings.

I recognize the song she's singing. It's an old one, but not one of ours. It's a Beatles song. Except she is singing it slower in a real high voice and with the beat of a traditional Penacook greeting song. Like the ones that would be sung to travelers coming back from a long, hard trip. Somehow, strange as that may sound, it all adds up. And every other verse she pauses and sings:

Kwey-ah-hey, hey ah hey
Kwey-ah-hey, kwey-ah-hey.

I open my eyes and smile.

When I walk into the kitchen, Doda is just coming back in the front door. He has his cane in one hand and a little plate in the other. He only needs his crutches when he is going to walk a long way. Around the house he just uses the cane he carved out of a tree root. The handle is shaped like an eagle's head, with its head painted white, a yellow beak, and a black-feathered neck. The eyes are little shiny black stones. When he walks with it, that eagle's head faces forward and it looks like he is holding a little eagle in his hand.

Seeing the empty plate in his hand, I know it is okay to sit right down and eat. Auntie has put plates full of food on the table for all four of us. Celeste is sitting and waiting, her knife and fork in her hands. She is always hungry. Doda swings down into his ladder-back chair, hanging his cane on the peg in the wall behind him. Auntie takes the little plate, swishes it through the warm dishwater, rinses it, dries it, and places it in the dish drainer. All in one easy motion. Less time than it takes to count from one to three. Then she covers the drainer with a dish towel to keep the dry dishes clean and keep anything bad away from them.

When Mom was alive, we always said grace before we ate. We don't do that with Doda and Auntie. Doda already said thanks outside, the old way. That plate held a little bit of everything we were about to eat. I knew he had placed the food from the plate in the spot by the base of the mountain ash tree. Always have a mountain ash near your house because the mountain ash protects you, Doda says. The food from the plate was to be shared with the Manogies, the little people. They're the ones who keep watch over things. They like people who remember to share.

Do I really believe in Manogies? I sure do when I

am back at Penacook. Have I ever seen the little guys come and eat that food Doda puts out for them? Well, the food always disappears. And I have watched.

Once I saw this black squirrel come down from a tree and pick up a piece of corn bread from that plate. The black squirrel stopped and looked over at me where I was hiding behind the old wooden wheelbarrow. It chirped like it was scolding me and then it bounced off. I never did see that black squirrel again. Maybe a hawk got it. When you look different from the other squirrels, you can attract trouble.

But Auntie says that the little guys can take different shapes. Birds. Animals. Even bees. And some people have seen the way they look when they think no one is watching them. Then they look like little Indians. If you do see them that way, it is kind of like a gift. You're not supposed to tell anyone that you have seen them, though. If you tell anyone, then you will never, ever, see the Manogies again for the rest of your life. But they are still there, taking care of things.

Doda told me a story. The end of Penacook Lake that is part of our little reservation is really pretty. Prettier than any other part of the lake, with our island and everything. The rest of the lake is all state land. Ten years ago someone wanted to develop our end of the lake. He had a lot of money. Mr. Money, Doda called him.

Mr. Money figured if he could get a wide new road in here, then everything else would just fall into place. As it is, the two-lane road that runs from

Rangerville to the rez dead-ends here. But this guy's idea was to run the road right through and connect it up with the big state road ten miles on the other side of Penacook. It would cut us in half.

Mr. Money had friends in the state government. They liked his idea too. Our people didn't like it, but our Tribal Council was quiet. They were worried about making waves, so they didn't say yes or no. Then the surveyors arrived. They came right into Penacook, marking things down on paper and driving in stakes with red ribbons on them.

On the other side of town, where the road ends but where the new road was supposed to keep going, there is this hill. On the other side of it is a stone cliff. The road builders planned to go right through it with dynamite. The surveyors parked their trucks in front of St. Anne's Church and walked off with their instruments over the hill toward the cliff. About an hour later they all came running back. They'd lost their hats, and their instruments were broken. They were bruised and some of them were bleeding. No one asked them what had happened, but they told people anyway. A whole gang of little Indian kids dressed in old-time clothing had attacked them as soon as they hammered in the first stake near the cliff. Those little Indian kids threw rocks at them. They had really good aim! The surveyors had to run for their lives.

They weren't our kids, people told them. Our kids are all in school.

The Catholic priest, Father Benet, listened to them

talk from the top of the steps leading into the church. Then he just smiled and shook his head and went back into the church. He was new at Penacook then, but even he knew better than to walk over that hill to the cliff where the Manogies have a special place.

The surveyors left town and never came back. After that happened, the Tribal Council knew what they should do. They told the state they didn't want a new road. Mr. Money's highway never got built.

Looking across the table as I pour some maple syrup on my pancakes, I see Doda smiling at me. I wonder if he knows I am remembering the story he told me about how that road never got built. I feel happy now. It is so good to be in this little house. And this little town of a thousand people and a hundred houses and trailers and one store and one little school and one little church and one tribal meeting hall is such a good place. When I am here my heart feels almost whole.

I know that some of the people in this town are screwed up. No way are Indians perfect, and we Penacooks are no exception. Some drink a lot. Even some who are old and supposed to be elders. Not Doda and Auntie, but people like them. Husbands run away and don't take care of their families. Some of the kids not much older than me are into drugs, especially after a few years of going to the central school in Rangerville. Pot and glue-sniffing. People in Penacook get beat up and hurt and lost and angry, just like people anywhere. But there's something else here that was so hard to remember when I was with Mito in Boston that first year after Mom died. Something that we were once and something that some of us still can be. It's in the earth and the wind and in the water. It's in the memories that the little guys keep for us.

After breakfast I walk outside. It rained last night and washed everything clean. I like when it rains on a Friday night. Then the weekend is a whole new thing. The rain washes away the bad tastes of a week in Rangerville. Like when you rinse your mouth out with fresh water after eating something you didn't like.

The rain has washed the heaviness out of the air. I like the taste of the air now. It is one of those September mornings when you feel like you are going to live forever. On Saturday you can almost believe that.

I pull the bike that was my dad's out of the shed. Its tires are as skinny as fingers, not like the trail bikes everybody rides now. It weighs a ton too. But I like it. It feels solid and I feel solid when I get on it. And it is downhill from our house into the rest of town. I can look back in the other direction and see a little of the water through the trees. I'll go there later, maybe, if Gartersnake and the other guys are free.

But first I check with Doda to see if he needs help. He is sawing wood in the back, filling up the green wood woodshed. We have two big woodsheds that face each other right out the back door. Both are almost full. The green wood woodshed is for next year. The wood in it has to dry until the ends of the logs have little cracks in them and they are just right for burning. Then the other woodshed will become the green wood woodshed.

Doda moves slow, but he is steady, like a turtle. I love the way he gets the wood in. We don't make a mess in the woods, like the loggers who get their permits to cut on the state land on the other side of the rez. They come in with big machines and when they are done, there are gouge marks on the earth, broken trees that weren't quite right for the sawmill discarded by the roadsides. Giant raggedy piles of brush. There are empty white plastic chainsaw-oil bottles, beer cans, candy wrappers, cigarette packs all over. It looks like some giant messy kid with a bad temper went through, swatting at the forest and dumping trash in every direction.

Today Doda is using his crosscut saw to cut the small lengths into eighteen-inch logs for the stove. Less waste with a crosscut. Doesn't use gas and oil.

"I cut now," he says, "you stack later." He points with his chin down the hill. That means I should go ahead and do what I want.

I check out Celeste before I go. I always do that, let her know where I am going. She acts like she's not paying attention to me, but I know whenever I turn my back her eyes are staring at me. She's playing with Buffy St. Mary, her copper-skinned doll.

It is actually Pocahontas, but Auntie and Celeste did some work on her. A Penacook makeover.

They padded the waist so that, as Auntie put it, "She looks like a woman and not some danged ant." Then they dumped the corny buckskin miniskirt.

"She dress this way," Auntie said, "her knees gonna be all scarred from the blackberry bushes."

They gave her a nice long ribbon dress, like the one Auntie wears when we have the summer ceremonial day.

Then Celeste renamed her after the Cree lady she used to watch on *Sesame Street*, Buffy Sainte-Marie, and the Virgin Mary. Celeste likes them both and so she put their names together. Auntie has a television, just a small one, but it gets all the channels because Mito put up a satellite dish the last time he was home. I watch it more than anyone else does.

"Celeste," I say, "I'm gonna look for the guys. Want to come?"

I can balance her sideways on the bike between my arms. No problem. But she shakes her head and holds up the doll. "Me and Buffy are too too busy."

"Kwey-kay," I say. It is a word that Gartersnake and Pizza and Belly Button and I made up. It combines okay, which Doda tells me is actually an Indian word—Choctaw, I think—and *kwey*. *Kwey* sort of means "hi" in Penacook. I strap my stick onto the luggage carrier on the back of the bike, do a short wheelie—which is hard to do with an English bike—and I'm out of there.

I don't get far down the hill before I hear the yell.

"Incoming!"

I squeeze the rear handbrake—the only one that works. The bike skids sideways as I thrust one leg out for balance. With my other hand I have pulled the stick off the luggage carrier and I've got it up just in time.

Thwap! The hard white ball that was hurled out of the bushes is caught in the net of my lacrosse stick.

Gartersnake stands up.

"Almost got you that time, Tonto," he says.

I throw the ball back at him so hard that he ducks instead of catching it with his own stick. My arms may be skinny, but they're long and I can really whip.

"Hey!" he says. He looks hurt. I'm already sorry. He and I have been friends longer than anybody. Ever since he bit me when his mom was baby-sitting for me and we were both crawlers.

"Don't ever call me that again," I say.

He closes one eye like he usually does before he is going to say something. I know what he is going to say. I'm sorry that he is going to say it.

"At least you look Indian."

I don't answer that. Our friendship depends on my not answering that. Gartersnake's mom is Penacook, but his dad is Norwegian. A foreign exchange student who left something extra behind after spending his senior year in high school in Rangerville. An Indian baby with brown skin, blond hair, and blue eyes. The guy never answered the letters that Gartersnake's mom wrote to him. Probably married some-body named Sigrid. Paddles around on the fjords be-ing chased by trolls and reindeer.

To make things worse, Gartersnake's mom named him Sven. It was a name that no one spoke, under pain of death. Even his mother never called him that anymore. He stopped eating for four days the last time she did that, when he was seven. Even his teachers in Rangerville always referred to him solely by his last name: Mr. Dana. Or just Dana.

Gartersnake or just plain Snake is the name that we call him. It comes from his Indian name, which is "Striped Snake That Bites." It is sort of a secret name just between us friends, the way they call me "Bridge" sometimes.

I lay my bike down and go help Gartersnake find the lacrosse ball. We're quiet as we look. We know that sticks and stones hurt a lot less than names do. Finally Gartersnake finds it wedged under a tree root that is arched like a yellow hand with its fingers dug back into the earth. He holds it up.

"Kwey-kay, Bridge," he says.

"Kwey-kay, Snake," I answer. Friends again.

When we get to the church steps, our usual Saturday morning meeting place, Pizza and Belly Button are there. They both have their sticks across their laps. Belly Button is as round as I am skinny. As far as his nickname goes, if you ever went swimming with him you'd get it. Like a thumb! Belly Button is living proof of the fact that Penacooks adopted all kinds of other Indians into our tribe. I don't know if any of them got this far north way back when, but he looks just like a Pueblo Indian. Short, stocky, and tough as shoe leather.

Just like his dad and mom. Of the three of us Belly Button is the only one who has an actual mother and father both alive and living together. They really seem to like each other too. So the four of us spend a lot of time at their place. It's a double-wide trailer on Turtle Street, the little muddy lane off the main road. It is always wet down there. Frogville, folks call that part of the rez. Or Mosquito Town in the summer. There is so much water there that every trailer has its own ice rink in the backyard when winter comes. Even Turtle Street itself turns into ice, and you can skate on it most of the winter—as long as you watch out for the four-wheelers. From December to March we skate more than we walk. Belly Button's family, him and his parents and his grandparents and his five brothers and sisters who all live together in that double-wide along with five dogs and several thousand cats, always make the biggest and best skating rink and keep it nice and clear with a snowplow on the front of their four-wheeler.

Pizza is a year older than the rest of us, and four inches taller than me, but he's in the same grade. He got held back for attitude. Pizza's dad was Penacook, but his mom was African American. No one knows what happened to his mom. Somebody said it had something to do with drugs. His dad was killed in the army while he was in the Middle East. Pizza has very thick, reddish-colored, curly hair. I guess he must look some like his mom did. Or still does. He lives with his dad's sister and her kids. They treat him pretty good. But Pizza, who hardly ever speaks more than one word at a time, has a lot of, you know, attitude. He doesn't like to hang around there. And I bet you know what he likes to eat better than anything else. Hot dogs. (Just kidding.)

The four of us, because we hang out together and all look so different, have our own nickname. We get called the Rainbow Coalition. We shortened it to the Coalition.

Pizza unfolds himself and hops down the steps on one foot. Belly Button comes tumbling after him like a Slinky going down the stairs.

" 'Sup?" Pizza says.

"Kwey-kay?" Belly Button asks, brushing himself off and smiling as he jumps back up to his feet. If you threw Belly Button against a wall he'd just bounce back like a lacrosse ball.

"Kwey-kay," all four of us say together.

We go over to the ball field behind the church. There is a net set up there for lacrosse or field hockey or soccer. We pass the ball around for a few minutes and then play some two-on-two. After we all have bloody noses, we figure we've played enough for a while. Unless everybody is bleeding you haven't really been playing lacrosse Penacook-style.

"Lake?" Pizza asks.

"Kwey-kay."

By the time we get to the lake and pull our bikes up on the shore, the sun is right in the middle of the sky. The leaves are turning on the island, but the water is still as warm as August. There won't be too many more days like this. The wind blows wicked hard up here in early autumn. Anybody who has managed to grow a garden has to harvest everything in early September if they want to make sure to beat the hard frost.

Pizza sees them first.

"Man!" he says, like he just stepped in a big pile of dog poop.

"Oh, no!" Gartersnake groans.

"Oh, yes," Belly Button sighs. "This is bum!"

I don't say anything. I am feeling sick. There are stakes and flags everywhere. I don't know when they put them in, probably while we were all in school at Rangerville. Some of our favorite trees here—and out on the island—have yellow or red ribbons tied around them. The surveyors have been here. Red means cut down. Yellow means leave for effect.

Like everyone else, I've heard the talk about the casino that is being planned for our rez. I've even thought some about the pros and cons of it. How it would bring jobs into the community on the one hand and how gambling can mess people up on the other. But I've never thought about where they might actually put it. Not here, not on our island. If they put a casino on it, there will be nothing left!

Where are the little guys when we really need them? I'm thinking. But I already know. The Manogies are probably disgusted with us because we are going to do this to ourselves. It's not some Mr. Money in another city with big plans. It is us Penacooks.

Doda and Auntie didn't tell me about this. About the surveyors already staking the island out. Are we going to just let them do this? But I know it isn't the decision of our family alone. Although we're the ones who have always taken care of the island, it belongs to the tribe on paper.

Our new chief, going back and forth to the state capital in his business suit and with his briefcase, says that we need development. Then we can provide jobs. Have an alcohol and drug treatment center, build a bigger school, have full employment. "Root out despair, return to pride." That was his slogan when he won the elections.

"Huh!" Pizza says, the same disgust still there in his voice. He is kicking at one of the stakes.

"What are we going to do now?" Gartersnake says.

"Get in trouble," I say. I start pulling up stakes.

"Kwey-kay," the guys say. We pull up every stake we can find. We take Doda's boat and go out to the island and pull up the stakes there. We take the ribbons off the trees and row everything back to shore. Then we make a fire on the beach and we burn all the stakes in it. There's a lot of smoke rising. Probably too much. We should have taken the plastic flags off the stakes first. We hear a siren from the direction of our little firehouse, which is next to the church. The whole fire department has one truck and six volunteer firemen.

"Run?" Pizza says. He's looking at me like I'm the leader now. I'm surprised. Not just at the way he and the other guys look at me, but at the way I respond. My voice sounds a lot more sure of itself than my stomach is.

"No," I say. My feet want to run as the siren gets closer, but I dig the toes of my sneakers into the sand. "We did it. Now we wait here and tell them why we did it."

I sit down and the other three members of the Coalition sit with me in a circle around our fiery protest.

We are in big trouble.

4 Talking

The first to arrive are four volunteer fireguys. When they see it is just a bonfire, they don't even bother to put it out. It's been pretty well burned down by the time they get to the beach, anyhow. Those dry pine stakes burn hot. The men stand there with us just looking at the fire, none of us saying anything, all of us waiting. Then we hear it, the rumble of the engine of the tribal cruiser and the crunch of its tires on the stones above the beach.

We all look up. Just as I expected, Kojak and Barney Fife are in the tribal patrol car. Those aren't really their names. They are Penacooks like the rest of us. But they were given those nicknames years ago. Kojak was some bald detective on television back when our Kojak joined the force, and Barney Fife was a skinny country deputy who'd been on some other show. Doda says you can still see the real Kojak and Barney Fife on reruns, but most of us under the age of twenty just think of our Kojak and our Barney Fife as the only ones with those names. So we don't get the joke, Doda says.

Kojak, who is the tribal police chief, is also my dad's cousin. I call him Uncle Buster. His real name is Buster Nicola. He has hair down to his shoulders. He always has a lollipop stick in his mouth. Doda says that is because the original guy on TV always used to suck on a lollipop. Uncle Buster doesn't like lollipops, so he takes the candy off them first. He gives the candy to his kids. He just chews the sticks. He eases out of the car and motions to Barney Fife to get out too.

"We got a hot one, Sam," he says.

Barney Fife does not look anything at all like the guy on TV, according to Doda. He isn't little and skinny and goofy. He doesn't have a high-pitched voice. He's a natural baritone. He is tall and good-looking. Real muscular, lifts weights. When everyone started calling him Barney Fife, a name he did not like, he began lifting even more weights. He is now built like Hulk Hogan. But because he is the other half of the Penacook Police Department, and therefore the deputy, people still call him Barney Fife. Even though his name is Sam Sabael.

When Uncle Buster and Sam join us, they don't say anything either. They just look at the fire, then at the lakeshore and the island clean of surveyors' stakes and ribbons. It does look better now. I think they see that. They look at us, then they look at each other. Nobody saying nothing.

Uncle Buster takes a lollipop stick out of his shirt pocket and puts it into the corner of his mouth. He looks at me and shakes his head. Then he turns to Sam.

"What do you think, Sam? Should we read 'em their rights?"

Sam looks back at Uncle Buster and opens his mouth. But he never gets a chance to answer, because that is when I start talking. And for some reason, when I start talking, everyone else gets even quieter and listens. I don't know how long everyone listens. Time has a way of going away when I start talking like this. Nervous energy, my aunt calls it. And she is usually right about that. But this time when I am talking, I feel different.

I look over at Gartersnake and Pizza and Belly Button. I don't stop talking, I just use my peripheral vision. Their eyes are wide and they are staring at me. Gartersnake's mouth is open. I am talking in both Penacook and English now.

The four fireguys and the two tribal police are just staring at me too, as I jabber and wave my arms. I think I must look like Daffy Duck having a fit. But I don't shut up.

I tell them how we don't own this land. All of us Penacooks belong to it. So we have no right to do what is planned here. There should never be anything built here. The land will not like it. The island has to stay the way it is because it is our heart. It beats like a drum. I say it in Penacook.

I don't say much in Penacook, but every time I do, all of the adults look at me and then look at each other. I hear one of the fireguys say "Unh-hunh" a couple of times. The fire has now burned down to ashes and I am still going. There is this circle around me of my three friends and the four firemen and the two tribal policemen. All listening.

Finally, I pause for breath. Uncle Buster nods to Sam. Sam picks me up with one arm like I'm a little kid. Not rough, just kind of swooping me up. As soon as he has picked me up, I start talking again. Sam carries me up to the patrol car while I look back over his shoulder, my eyes on the island.

"The Grandmothers all told us to take care of our island," I say.

"That's right," Sam says in a soft voice, but he doesn't stop walking.

Our island. Our island. I am still talking when Sam lowers me into the car and then climbs into the backseat with me. Uncle Buster, chewing thoughtfully on his lollipop stick, closes the door.

When the door shuts, it is like a switch is clicked off inside me. I stop talking. Sam lets go of me and I slump down on the seat next to him like a normal kid. A normal kid who has been busted. Things are so quiet inside the car that I can hear the sound of the tires on the gravel road as we go up the hill. I think they might keep going with me, take me down to the tribal building, have some kind of trial and then put me into jail. But they don't.

They stop in front of Doda and Auntie's house. My house. Uncle Buster gets out of the car first. Before he shuts the door, he turns around and looks at me.

"Chris, you stay here now. You hear me?"

I nod. I stay there and Sam stays there with me. We wait while Uncle Buster goes inside. The sun is shining down on the roof of the cruiser. Sam pushes the button on his armrest. *Whirrrrrr.* The window rolls down on his side. He looks over at me. I push my button and watch my window whir down too. Then we wait some more.

Sam hums a drum song. He begins to flex his biceps, making them bounce up and down in time with the song. I try to flex my arm muscles, but all I can do is move my elbow in and out. We keep on waiting.

When Uncle Buster comes out he is laughing. But when he sees I am looking at him he stops and looks very serious. He comes over and opens my door. I get out. He puts his hand on my shoulder.

"You gonna do that again, Chris?"

"I won't," I say.

Then he gets back into the car. Sam squeezes himself out of the back. Before he climbs in front with Uncle Buster, Sam flashes me a peace sign and pumps his biceps muscle a couple more times. Some people might call him Barney Fife, but Sam Sabael is cool.

When I go inside, Auntie and Doda are waiting for me. They don't say anything about what has happened. They want me to have time to consider everything that has occurred before they talk to me about it. They wait and I wait. Night comes and I go to bed. When I wake up, it is Sunday morning. Time for Mass.

Auntie walks ahead as she always does. I stay

back with Doda, who moves slow with his crutches. When the hill gets slippery in winter, he lets someone drive him. But while the weather is warm he prefers to walk, even though it takes us an hour to get back home.

Partway up the hill the road winds so that you can get a glimpse of the lake. Gluskabe's Seat is there. Mito said to me once that he used to sit on that same seat when he was a kid. Doda says that seat has always been right there, since the world was made. Doda and I sit down on the stone seat. It is nice and warm from the morning sun. I know he is going to talk to me now about what I did.

Doda directs his gaze toward the lake. I look that way too. A big bird is circling over there, an eagle. There is a big nest in the tallest pine on the island. The eagle circles higher and higher and then it is lost in the sun.

Doda turns his head back. He takes one of his crutches and taps a stone with it. I look at that stone. It is smooth and round and shiny. There is no other stone like it here, just blue gravel and brown earth and that one round stone. It is just like one of the stones on the beach of our island. Then Doda says my name. The long version of it in Penacook. I look up at him.

"My grandson," he whispers, "stones don't get impatient."

"Unh-hunh," I answer. I pick up that stone. I am pretty sure that is what he wants me to do. He nods and I put it in my pocket.

"Help you remember," he says in his normal voice. Then he levers himself up and starts walking. The talk is over. That is all he is going to say.

When we get to the church, though, other people are saying more. The thing about living on a reservation is that everybody knows what everybody else is doing. And everybody talks about it. Gossip is one reason why some of our people move away from Penacook. They just can't stand it that someone is always looking over their shoulder. That is what my dad says was his reason for moving away. But I know it was more than that. Mito has other reasons to stay away from us.

As Doda and Auntie and I walk into church, a lot of people turn to look at me. Some look over at me and nod and smile. Other people whisper and then pointedly look the other way. The chief and his wife just stare straight ahead like they were carved out of stone.

Among Indians, people don't usually go around telling you what to do. We don't generally come up to someone and say do this or don't do that. We don't like to interfere with each other. Not directly. But everybody has an opinion about what you do.

When church is over, I walk outside and see my friends. Belly Button is with his parents. On the other side of the crowd Pizza is leaning on his bike talking with Gartersnake. I head toward them. Gartersnake runs when he sees me coming and Pizza just rides his bike right by me. I stand there, feeling confused. Someone takes me by the arm.

"Chris, come with us," Belly Button says. His mom and dad are close behind him. I look over at Doda and Auntie. Doda nods and Auntie waves her fingers.

As we walk, Belly Button's parents talk to me. I haven't realized until now how divided our people are about the idea of the casino. I'd thought most folks saw it as a good thing.

"You see how Father Benet paused and smiled at you when he put the communion wafer on your tongue?" Belly Button's dad says.

"The only gambling he wants to see at Penacook is church bingo," says Belly Button's mom.

I find myself remembering how as I left church a couple of grown-ups had patted me on my back, while others turned their backs on me.

As Belly Button's parents talk, I realize for the first time how some people feel that a casino is against our traditional way of life. It is not right to gamble.

"And a casino will divide us," Belly Button's dad says. Then he explains how he has seen what has happened on some reservations with casinos when the people running them hadn't been honest. A lot of the money had gone off the rez. Gone to the Mafia. A few Indian people got big trucks and new houses. Most people got nothing. There had even been a little tribal war over casinos among the Mohawks ten years ago. The Antis and the Pros had picked up guns against each other. Some people got killed.

I am too young to remember any of what they are talking about, but I am learning an awful lot about it this Sunday afternoon.

"What you did, Chris," Belly Button's mom says as we turn down Turtle Street, "it woke everyone up. It brought things out into the open."

We are at their double-wide now. We go inside and Belly Button's mom motions for me and Belly Button to sit down on the couch.

"I just made some frybread this morning," she says. "I'll get some for you boys. I know you're always hungry."

Belly Button's dad has disappeared somewhere into the back of the trailer. I hear boxes being moved. Then he comes out with something in his hand. It is a braid of sweetgrass. He hands it to me.

"You know," he says, "we say that sweetgrass chases away bad things."

I hold his gift in my hand and look at the plate of frybread that has been put down on the little coffee table in front of us.

"You see, Chris?" Belly Button's dad says. "You see how it is?"

Belly Button reaches out for a piece of frybread, spoons some honey onto it, and starts to eat. But I can't eat. All I can do is hold on to the sweetgrass braid with both hands. Belly Button's parents are so serious. Their voices are so soft and insistent as they continue to talk to me that it spooks me. It scares me. I stay scared. What have I started?

5 The Chiefs

I'm sitting in the school library. It is Friday afternoon, the third week in September. When you are in school and it is Friday afternoon and you're waiting for the school week to be over, you can get the feeling that it will never end. Friday afternoon lasts forever.

Usually I like being in the library. I always try to pick up at least one new word every time I go. Like the time I got the word peripheral. Relating to the surrounding space, the edges. Good one for me. Today, though, I haven't even gone over to the dictionary. I'm only pretending to read the book in front of me on the library table. I've been trying to catch the eye of my friends.

Gartersnake is over near the window. He finally started talking to me again this week. I know I scared him with all the stuff I said back after we burned the surveyors' stakes. But now things are almost back to normal between us. Except Gartersnake has his nose buried in the Goosebumps section and he doesn't notice me looking at him.

Because there's been too much talking in the library, we are under strict orders to get a book and sit with it whenever we come in here for library time. So even though it is the only time when all of us who used to be together in the Coalition are in one place in school, we really can't talk.

Pizza is sitting right across from me, close enough to whisper or pass a note. But Pizza has stopped communicating with the three of us—anywhere. Pizza's aunt, who he lives with, is really in with the casino crowd. She resents anyone who is even remotely anti-casino. She doesn't want him to talk to me.

He is also totally involved with football. He went out for the modified team and everyone says that he's doing great. He's on the first-string. Right now he is reading a book about the life of Jim Thorpe, the Mesquakie Indian athlete. I kick his leg under the table, but he just scoots his chair further back.

Belly Button would look at me. But Belly Button is buried in the book he's reading at the other end of the library. It just came in and it's about whales. He loves whales and is doing a report on them. I look over at Pizza again. No response.

Pizza is completely involved in football. Immersed in it. Drowned.

It was just two days after we made our bonfire on the beach from the surveyors' stakes that Pizza joined the modified football team at Rangerville. I don't understand much about modified football. I've never been a football fan. But I've been told that modified football is like regular football, with the rules just a little simpler so that it is easier for the junior high kids to play it.

But whether it is the junior high or the high school team, the team name is the same. And that is what really bugs me. They call themselves the Rangerville Chiefs. They paint their cheeks like phony Indians before every game and shout out war whoops when they take the field. Lots of people on the Rangerville side join in, and they also do the tomahawk chop like on television. Sometimes, especially for the high school games, the kids make up signs with ugly cartoon Indians on them holding tomahawks. SCALP 'EM, CHIEFS, the signs read.

But Pizza hasn't let that bother him. Pizza has about given up on being a Penacook. Be a Chief instead of being an Indian. He'd much rather be accepted by the other kids at school. And a lot of them seem to look up to the Chiefs. Pizza is not the first. Other Penacook kids have joined the Chiefs in the past. Right now, though, Pizza is the only Penacook kid in modified football. When the bell rings, he scoots out of his chair and is out of the door before I can even close the book I've been pretending to read. Today is the first game and he has to get suited up.

As we walk out of school with our backpacks, Belly Button and I talk about it.

"It is worse by the time you get to high school,"

Belly Button says. "The Rangerville High School team is called the Big Chiefs." Then he goes on to describe how their mascot, who is never a real Indian, dresses in buckskin with a Plains Indian headdress and runs up and down the sidelines leading people in the tomahawk chop. "Last year," he says, "the Big Chiefs went to the state finals. Whooping all the way."

But Pizza doesn't seem to mind. I've never seen him so set on anything before. Usually, all he wants to do is kid around, but he is so serious now. Just the way he was reading that book, *really* reading it because it is about a football player, was different. I can tell how much it all means to him. And a part of me is glad for him, even though I'm worried. What if he blows it? What if he doesn't do well? Will he come back to being the old Pizza we used to know, our buddy who didn't really care about much of anything except our little group of friends? Or will he just give up on everything?

As I'm thinking about this, Gartersnake comes up to us.

"Hey, guys, I just found out they got this special late bus so that kids can go to the football game," he says. "Want to go?"

Belly Button looks at me and I nod my head.

The football field where the junior high plays is right behind the school. There are wooden bleachers on either side instead of a big grandstand like the one on the high school field. The junior high scoreboard has to be changed by hand. It isn't electronic like the one for the high school. But even though everything is on a smaller scale, it hasn't kept people from coming to this game. It isn't just kids, there are loads of teachers and parents and even people from the surrounding towns who don't have kids in school. I haven't realized until now how serious a thing football is here. It is a hot and sunny autumn afternoon and everybody is talking loud. The smell of sweat and spilled soft drinks and hot dogs cooking makes me think of the county fair in the summer.

There are a dozen cheerleaders wearing the school colors. I recognize a couple of them from my class, girls who are really popular. I hadn't known they were cheerleaders, but it figures. I stop and look, trying to see if I recognize any of the other girls. I don't. Katie isn't one of them. I feel relieved. I don't want her to be a cheerleader. Then I see her. She is standing up in the stands and I can see her long black hair and her profile.

And then I feel this impulse to go over to her. For the last two weeks I've been avoiding her in class, not looking her way even when I can feel her looking over at me. But now, for some reason, I feel different. I want to tell Katie I am sorry for laughing with my friends about her being a Cherokee Princess. Even though she doesn't know I did it, I feel like I should apologize to her. But my feet won't move. People are bumping into me. Belly Button tugs my sleeve.

"Bridge," he says, talking loud to be heard over the noise of the crowd, "come on."

When I look down at him, it breaks the spell. My feet can move again. Something inside me isn't happy about it, but I've made the decision not to try to talk to Katie today, not with everyone around like this. The three of us, Belly Button, Gartersnake, and me, make our way over to the fence near the twenty-yard line. There are no seats in the bleachers on the home team side, and we aren't dumb enough to make the mistake of standing on the opposite side of the field. Somehow, in the midst of all this confusion, the teams have come out onto the field and the game is about to begin. A whistle blows and a football comes flying through the air toward the Chiefs' side of the field.

"That's Pizza!" Gartersnake whispers, his voice hoarse with excitement. And I can feel it too. There is a lump caught in my throat as the ball comes sailing down toward Pizza, who is standing there with his hands up, waiting to catch the ball and run. He looks small and skinny, even in the padded uniform that makes his shoulders twice as wide and the shiny new helmet that covers his head.

"He's gonna do it," Belly Button says, his hands held up in fists.

But he doesn't. The ball slips through Pizza's hands and thunks against his chest. Our groan is echoed by everyone around us. The ball bounces back and goes right into the hands of a player on the opposing team, who runs with it into the end zone. Pizza's mistake has just scored a touchdown for the other side.

People are booing as Pizza comes off the field.

"Stone hands!" someone yells.

I turn around in time to see a big, red-faced man in a New England Patriots jersey stand up in the front of the bleachers and shout, "Get that loser out of there."

I feel like I'm ready to cry, but as I watch Pizza leave the field, his head down, I see Coach Takahashi go over to him. He places both hands on Pizza's shoulders and leans forward so that his forehead touches Pizza's helmet. I can't hear what he is saying, but I see Pizza's back get straight again as he lifts his head to listen.

The other team doesn't succeed in making the extra point and they line up for another kickoff. To everyone's surprise, Pizza trots back onto the field to take the same place in the receiving team.

"NO!" People are yelling. "No, not him again!"

"Keep that kid out of there. Are you crazy, Coach?"

I don't turn around again to look at the people in the bleachers. I just watch Pizza. Gartersnake and Belly Button and I watch him and hold our breaths as the ball floats up, so slow that it looks like a lopsided balloon, and heads right for him. But this time he catches it. He steps aside from the first tackler, bounces off a second one, picks up a block and gets over to the sidelines, and then he begins to run. He runs the way we Penacook kids know he can run, faster than a deer. The boos have turned into cheers as he reaches the end zone and then stops to hold the ball over his head for just a second before he flips it to a referee. Touchdown.

People are going crazy on our side of the field. A bunch of kids are doing the tomahawk chop while others are patting their hands against their mouths to do phony war whoops.

The cheerleaders are doing cartwheels. They hold up their pom-poms and sing out together, "TONY, TONY, HE'S OUR MAN. IF HE CAN'T DO IT, NO ONE CAN!"

Just as I realize they are talking about Pizza—Anthony is his given name, which no one at Penacook ever uses—the big man in the New England Patriots jersey stands up. "Scalp 'em, Injun, scalp 'em!" he bellows. Other people take up his chant.

"SCALP 'EM, INJUN, SCALP 'EM."

I realize for the first time what it is like to be excited and depressed all at once. I look at my friends and see the same look on their faces that must be on mine. Should we laugh or cry?

The Rangerville Chiefs win the game. Pizza scores two more touchdowns, running down the field with the same zigzag grace he showed when the four of us played lacrosse together and none of us could ever catch him.

In the second half, after he scores the third touchdown, he looks over at us standing near the fence.

Gartersnake, Belly Button, and me. The only three people on our side of the field not chanting and doing the tomahawk chop. He nods and holds the ball over his head. Like he is sharing it with us.

When the gun sounds, ending the game, people run onto the field. Some of them lift Pizza up for a moment on their shoulders and he looks around as if trying to see us. But we are invisible. We watch as he disappears, running toward the school locker room with the other football players. Gartersnake and Belly Button and I sit there for a long time. I think all of us feel the way I do. Proud and empty at the same time.

It is late at night. I'm not sure how late. I look up at the ceiling. I wish that my dad were here. When Mito is sober, he can talk about things like this with me. He could make me laugh. He could help me understand how I am feeling now about Pizza and Katie, about our island and the casino. I close my eyes, trying to see Mito's face.

The first ring of the phone wakes me up before I realize I've been sleeping. It rings twice more before Auntie comes out and gets it. She says hello first in English. Then she makes that little sound she makes when she is delighted. Then, in Penacook, she says, "My grandchild." And I know who it is. My dad. Sometimes old people call a younger person grandchild when they're not really related by blood. But the way Auntie said "my grandchild," I knew. She only says it that way to my dad. He is her favorite.

I am wide awake. But I don't move. I'm afraid that I might be dreaming and just imagining he has called, and I'm afraid that he really is on the phone and that he has been drinking again. It is so scary when that happens. Because then it is him and it isn't him. It's like one of those body-snatcher movies where the person you know and love is gone and has been replaced by some cold alien being that just seems to be your sister or your husband or your father.

I remember what it was like the last time.

"Tell 'em I need money, you hear me!"

That was what he said when I answered the phone. It was summer. Two months before I went back to school. Before I burned the stakes and almost started a war at Penacook.

I was baby-sitting Celeste while Doda and Auntie were down at the church. I could hear a woman laughing somewhere in the background and the *whoom-a-whoom-a-whoom* of trucks going by. He was calling from a phone booth in front of a bar.

"You take down this number. Western Union. Have them send the money here. Code name Grizzly Bear. You hear me."

But he didn't give me the number. He just kept saying the same things in that alien voice. Cold. Mean. Again and again, but getting softer as he spoke. His voice sad now.

And that was when I hung up the phone. Just as Doda and Auntie had told me I should do.

After I hung up, I said, "I love you, Mito."

When they got home a little later, Doda and Auntie told me I did the right thing. A week after that they told me that Mito had checked into a good program. He was going to try. Celeste smiled when they told us that. But she didn't say anything. Neither did I. We had heard that he was going to try before. He'd been trying ever since Mom died.

She was on her way home with groceries that night. It wasn't late, but it was dark. She didn't see the black ice on the road and her car went out of control, down the hill and into the trees. I remember someone saying that the only good thing about it was that no one was with her. The way the car was smashed up, anyone else in it would have died with her. Maybe that was true, but it was as if something died in all of us after the crash. And even though he tried for a while to take care of us, it was clear that Mito had lost the most. Part of him was empty, and he tried to cover over that empty place with drinking.

Since that last phone call we hadn't seen or heard from him. Auntie said that was a good sign. He was concentrating on the program. He had to find himself again before he could come back to us.

Then, tonight, the phone rang.

Auntie is listening to him. Every now and then she says something.

"Yes. That is good. Going good."

I try to imagine what Mito's voice sounds like. I think it must sound stronger again, more like himself. I want to feel happy. But for some reason I feel really anxious. It's like watching someone cross a high wire between two tall buildings. You can see they're halfway across. Their balance looks good. They know what they are doing. But if they make one wrong step, if a strong wind comes up all of a sudden . . .

Now Mito must be asking questions, because Auntie is doing most of the talking. It is about Doda first.

"Blood pressure good now. Those headaches not so bad now."

What headaches, I think? But now she is talking about Celeste.

"No, she is fine. The teachers just love her."

There is a longer pause on Auntie's end. I'm next, I know. But what Auntie says doesn't sound like it is about me.

"Like a sagamon," she says. "That's how he talked, they say. Everyone had to listen. It touched their hearts. He heard the call. He carries so much."

She must be talking about Doda again. About what he said at the council meeting. But what did she mean about him hearing the call? He hasn't gotten out of bed yet, so I don't think he heard the phone. But now I know she is talking about me.

"Doing real well in classes. . . . Yes . . . No, not yet.

But he will. It takes a while to know people. You remember how you were, my grandchild."

For a minute I think I can actually hear Dad's voice. He is laughing. That real loud laugh of his just about shakes the walls. It makes me think about the stories Mito tells me about Laughing Louis, who lived not so long ago. Maybe only fifty years ago.

I always hear Mito's laugh when he tells me those funny stories about that old Indian man who laughed whenever things went wrong for him. Like the time someone gave him an old car with hornets inside.

"How does it run?" Laughing Louis asked.

"It buzzes right along," he was told.

He got in the car and started it up without noticing two important things. The first thing was that there was no inside door handle on the driver's side. The second thing was that some hornets had built their nest under the seat. Those hornets came buzzing out and started stinging while he tried to find the missing door handle. He finally crawled out the window. But as he crawled out, despite all those stings, he was still in a good mood.

"Boy," Laughing Louis said, "that car really does buzz along!" Then he laughed and laughed.

I'll bet that Laughing Louis's laugh sounded just like my father's big, happy laugh.

I listen, trying to hear more of Mito's voice. But he is not saying anything more. The call is about to end.

When we end a phone conversation we don't say

good-bye. It's an English word and there is no word for good-bye in Indian. Usually we just wish the other person a good journey. But this time Auntie says something different before she hangs up.

When Auntie speaks in English, sometimes her words aren't quite right. At least I know that is what my Language Arts teacher would say. Auntie has a Penacook accent and she has a hard time with letters like *F* and sounds like *sh*. Words like *Frenchman* come out as *Platzmon* in Penacook. And sometimes she leaves words out too. Instead of saying "I am going to go to town," she might say "I go town."

Some people would say she speaks broken English. But when she switches into Penacook, she speaks it with such beauty. Her voice gets stronger, even though it doesn't get louder. There is so much power in her voice when she speaks Indian. I am sure that everything around is listening to her then, the birds, the trees, the wind.

She ends the call in Penacook, saying to Mito, "We need you."

Except what she says means a lot more than that. It means that all of us, him included, need the person he really is.

I hear her hang up. She pads back into the room where Celeste is sound asleep. In the bed next to me Doda sighs and then rolls over. I guess he was listening too.

The call has made me think of so many things. I'm

trying to feel happy. But mostly I feel worried. I wonder if Doda's head is aching now. I wonder about what Auntie meant when she was talking to Mito about me.

I wonder when my father will find himself and bring the person he really is back to us all.

6 Coming Back

"*Kwey, nidobak!* Hey, buddies! Use it or lose it out there," Muskrat Mike says. "Start off this Saturday with a little Joanne Shenandoah. Then, seeing as how October is headin' in, it's time for Smashing Pumpkins again."

Most radio stations run different programming on weekends, but because KOOK is so small, Muskrat Mike is on every day, even Sundays, when he does a special local news show and plays classical music.

I lean over and turn the radio off. I pull on one sneaker, lace it and double tie it. The other one is lost. I finally find it on the bookshelf, behind my dictionary. I pick up my jean jacket and sit on the edge of the bed. Breakfast is waiting for me. I have heard the soft sounds that Auntie makes to let me know. The tap of a fork put down on the table. The clink of an orange-juice glass against a plate. I'm not ready to go in and eat. There is so much going on in my head that I can't think about my stomach, but I know I have to go in because they're waiting.

Auntie is smiling. Her round face seems to glow like the moon. Although Auntie is really old and her hair is completely white, her face is hardly wrinkled at all, except for the smile lines around the corners of her mouth. Smooth like the face of Grandmother Moon.

When we're together at the table she looks over at Doda and then at me. Celeste, who is sitting next to Auntie, tugs at her apron.

"Tell him," Celeste says.

Celeste's eyes are sparkling. Auntie has told her about Dad's phone call.

"You hear the phone last night," she says. It isn't a question.

"Unh-hunh," Doda says, and I echo him.

Auntie nods. Just as she thought. She picks up her fork and knife and starts to eat. Celeste pulls at her apron again.

"Aunt-eeee," Celeste says.

But Auntie pretends not to notice. She is about to burst, but she keeps on with her teasing.

"My sisssterrr," Doda says, drawing his voice out in a pleading way and making a funny face as he does it. It makes all of us start laughing—Auntie, Doda, me, even Celeste.

Auntie wipes her eyes with her apron and takes a deep breath. She looks around at our smiling faces.

"He's doing really good," she says. She knows she doesn't have to say who he is. She knows that we all know she is talking about Mito and the alcohol program he checked himself into. "Be home. Maybe November."

"To stay?" I ask.

"Just for a visit this time. Then, maybe."

When you are not used to getting them, little gifts can be so big. This one makes me feel as if I want to run and climb trees and flap my arms until I fly like an eagle. Although that small voice down inside is whispering that I shouldn't expect too much. He tried before and didn't make it. Why should this time be different? But it will. It has to be. It is like Auntie said. We all need him.

Not just our family in our house here. Penacook needs him. I haven't said much about Mito, I know. But once it looked like he would be chief here, like Doda had been. Before he started drinking so much.

I remember how Mito came back home the Christmas a year after Mom's death. He had been through rehab and he was supposed to be better. Auntie and Celeste were rolling out dough. They were talking about the Christmas cookies they were going to make.

"Tandy tanes," said Celeste, who was only three.

"Reindeer," Auntie said.

"Wittul snowmen," Celeste added, "an 'tars, wots a 'tars."

"Lots of stars," Auntie agreed.

It was going to be a good Christmas. Mito and I had gone for an evening walk. Just to give them room to cook. The snow crunched under our feet. The sky was full of stars and the moon made the cool air just glow with light. Our breath floated in the air like ghosts. I didn't know where we were headed. Then we were standing in front of the ghost house.

That was what the kids in Penacook called it then and they still call it that now. It used to be three stories tall before the fire. Now only half of it is there, blackened from the smoke and flames. Weeds and sumac and fire cherry grow around it. No one goes close to it. I didn't know this was where Mito was going. Even though I was little, I knew all about the place. I knew who died here. I remember wanting to tell Mito to take me back home. But I couldn't talk. Maybe it was because of the ghosts. The ghosts were talking to both of us and we couldn't help it.

I remember how Mito leaned on the split-rail fence that still circles the yard. That fence was new when the fire started.

On a reservation a house fire is a terrible thing. Our reservation has the one little fire truck, so we're better off than a lot of reservations, I guess, with our little tanker. But there are no fire hydrants, and the nearest other volunteer company is in Rangerville. In the winter, when the lake is frozen, you can't even fill the tank up when it gets empty. Once a fire gets going good, about all you can do is try to get the people out and then watch it burn. They say a fire in a trailer is even worse than in a wooden house. A trailer with its metal skin is just like an oven when it gets going. Flames shoot out of the windows like blowtorches. But a house fire is bad enough.

Christmastime was when it happened. The day before Christmas. Mito's aunt and uncle and his cousins were in that house. All my grandmother's relatives that I never got to meet. If my dad had been there, maybe I would never have lived. If he hadn't been late coming back from Boston, he and Mom would have been in that house and they might have burned up too. Because it happened a year before I was born, I would never have existed.

I wanted to run away from the ghost house. They had been my relatives, but I felt scared. Not of ghosts, but of the ghost voices that Mito can hear now when he looks at the burned-up house. I don't think that the ghost voices he hears are really the voices of my uncle and aunt and my cousins. They loved Mito and they would never have hurt him. But the ghost voices that really come from inside him— those are the ones that hurt him.

"Maybe it was the wiring," he said. "I always told my uncle I was going to rewire the house for him. Never got around to it."

He tapped his knuckles against the split rail of the fence. "Put this fence in for them, though. Dug out every hole and set every post." He hit the fence harder with his fist. "Fence like this doesn't keep out fire, does it?"

"Dad," I said. He didn't look at me. Then I tried it in Penacook. "*N'mitongwes*. My father."

He looked down at me. He couldn't see me. In the moonlight I could see that his eyes were already far away. A shooting star trailed down the sky behind him, like a shining tear across the sleeping face of heaven.

When we got back to the trailer, the plate of warm cookies was there. Snowmen, candy canes, reindeer, and stars. Lots of stars. Celeste was in bed in the other room. Mito reached over the plate of cookies to pick up the keys to the car.

Doda saw the look in his eye. "Tomorrow is Christmas," he said.

"Just going to get something I forgot," Mito said. "Stores in Rangerville are open late tonight."

"Niawasos," Auntie said in Penacook. It was her special name for Mito. It means "my bear."

It almost stopped him. But it didn't. He hunched his shoulders and went out the door. The three of us stood there listening to the car door open and close. We heard the engine start and then the sound of tires crunching snow and gravel. That sound got further and further away down the hill. Then it was silent. None of us said anything. We knew what stores were open late in Rangerville. The liquor stores. And he didn't come home for Christmas.

After breakfast Celeste sticks Buffy St. Mary in her backpack, head poking out so that she can watch everything, and leaves to go play with some friends.

A blue jay is calling just outside the window. Doda listens to it, like it is telling him what to do, and then looks over at me. I go outside to stand and look at Auntie's flower garden. Usually it looks bright and happy there. She plants the tall kinds of flowers with bright blossoms. Foxglove, delphiniums, hollyhocks. Lots of butterflies and hummingbirds come there. But it is autumn and most of the flowers have gone by. There was a real hard frost two nights ago, and what flowers were left are limp and blackened.

I feel fragile, like a piece of thin ice with cracks all through it. I hear the sound of Doda's crutches coming up behind me.

"Need some help," he says.

We go out back and he hands me the splitting ax. It is my favorite part of getting the wood ready for winter. He sets up the logs and I split them. I'm tall enough to have the right leverage for splitting with one stroke. I've been getting stronger this year, even though my arms are still skinny. But Doda has also taught me the right way to use an ax. You don't muscle it. You get the balance just right and you let the ax do its own work. *Whap-chunk.* The two halves of the split log leap apart. *Whap-chunk. Whap-chunk.* We don't hurry it, Doda and I. But we keep a nice even rhythm going, like a song.

By the time we are done, split pieces of wood are piled around us up to our knees. I'm smiling again and feeling tough and fierce. Doda and I work for another half hour or so stacking the wood. My arms and hands and legs and back feel hot from the exercise I've had, and I'm feeling like it is Saturday morning again. My favorite time.

Doda looks at the stacked wood and nods. That

nod of his says more than a hundred words of thanks. We have done well. No doubt about it. He looks over at me and I know what he is thinking. Do I want to go now and look for my friends? That's what I usually do around this time on a Saturday.

But instead I say, "Want to get the boat, Doda?"

He slides his crutches under his arms and we start off. I grab the oars from the wall of the wood-shed. We head down the hill. The day is warm. There's no wind, the clouds are still in the sky. There is no change of weather coming in right now. But there won't be too many more days like this one. The water is as blue as hope and the island shimmers like a dream in the sun.

The sun is two hands high above the hills by the time we get down to Doda's boat. He levers himself in, his crutches shoved under his seat. As always I push the boat out toward our island and jump in as it rocks on the smooth surface of the water.

"You," Doda says when we are in the boat.

So I take the oars and row. It is always farther out to the island than it looks. It seems some days like you could just throw a rock from the shore and reach the island with it. But it is really about a quarter of a mile out. And the island is bigger than it looks from the shore. When you get on the island and walk into the forest there, you can get lost for a while. Although if you walk far enough you will eventually come out on the shore.

Halfway across, Doda begins to talk.

"Our family," he says, "has always been known as a family that works for the people. Before things got to be like they are now, our family were the best hunters. Sometimes it was dangerous to go into the woods as a hunter. Sometimes people would get caught in winter storms and be unable to return. Sometimes people had accidents and never came home. Our family knew that, but it never stopped us from going out. It was our job. We always made sure everyone else had enough to eat before we ate anything ourselves."

Doda pauses and I nod, not saying anything.

He clears his throat as he looks back at the mainland. "But the old way of hunting for the people wasn't enough anymore. The people needed help in a different way. We had to hunt in new ways. That is why your father went off to college. With a Harvard M.B.A. he could help find ways to bring jobs to Penacook, get people off welfare and food stamps."

Doda looks over at me, his eyes looking right into me. It is one of those times when he knows what I am thinking and we are saying as much to each other with silence as we could with any words. I keep rowing. The creaking oarlocks seem to be speaking my thoughts.

What happened to Mito? What happened to Mito? What happened to Mito?

Doda coughs, clears his throat. "And though it is different what he did, it is still the same. And life is just as dangerous now for a hunter as it was in the old days. Your father has been caught in the storm, grandson. So he has been unable to make his way home. But it seems that he has begun to find the trail again. It seems that he is going to come back."

The bow of the boat slips up onto the beach. Even though I have tears in my eyes, I balance myself carefully so that I don't tip us over, then stand and jump out to pull the boat up. It's pretty easy to do, even with Doda sitting in the stern. The boat is strong, but it's light. A guide boat. Doda made it fifty years ago, back when he was the best hunting and fishing guide in the big woods, and it still looks new. When the boat is beached I help him out. For some reason he doesn't need the crutches when we're on the island.

Doda walks slowly up from the beach. As he walks, he holds out his hand to brush the tree trunks the way a person reaches out to take the hands of his friends. There are no stakes with numbers written on them or ribbons around trees. The surveyors haven't come back, but there was a big meeting about the casino idea two nights ago and I wonder if they'll be staking out the island again.

Doda places his hands on a birch tree for a minute. He always does this, and I think maybe it is so he can absorb some of the tree's strength. In the old days birches were the trees of the medicine men. The birch tree's white sides are marked with black shapes where branches have fallen off. Those shapes look like birds with their wings spread out. I've heard the story about the birch trees before, but Doda tells it anyway, and it's good to hear him tell it.

"Gluskabe put these marks on the birch tree long ago," Doda says. "See the shapes of the thunder eagle's wings here? Because the thunder eagle's shape is on this tree, we know it is Gluskabe's special tree."

I look around. This island is so calm and beautiful. I can breathe easier when I am out here away from everything that is confusing. But will it stay this way? Doda and I haven't talked about the latest casino meeting. I know he's been waiting for the right time to tell me about it, and I sense that this is the time.

"Is the island safe?" I ask.

Doda chuckles. "Turns out," he says, "those surveyors went in solely under orders from the chief. Even the Tribal Council hadn't been consulted. So there was a little yelling at the start of the meeting. Then I stood up and reminded them that was not the right way to start a meeting."

I smiled at the thought of Doda standing up. Even though he is no longer young, he still stands very tall when he wants to. He is like Gluskabe, who can seem to be the height of ordinary men and then grow to the height of a great pine tree. Because Doda is who he is, an elder in Penacook and from a sagamon family, I'm sure that everyone really listened to him.

People on the rez have always respected Doda and Auntie. In the old times a lot of my ancestors were chosen to be the sagamons. A sagamon, Doda says, is sort of like a chief. But not elected by voting. When you vote, majority rules and minority feels like fools. In the old days it was not good if even one person felt left out when people came together to make decisions.

"They got quiet then," Doda continues. "So I was able to start things the right way, with a prayer in Penacook. I kept it simple and then translated it into English so our chief could understand it."

I knew what kind of prayer Doda had spoken. It was a prayer of thanks for all the gifts of life that people take for granted, for the earth and the water, the air and the trees, the birds and animals, all our friends and relatives. I know that he spoke it in a way that made people aware of all those gifts. And I am certain that he also spoke about the island as one of those special gifts that we must appreciate.

"After that," Doda says, "some of the anger that got so hot when you kids burned those surveyors' stakes cooled off. Our chief, he backed down some. He acted more like a chief, like a sagamon, than a politician. He agreed that nothing should be done until there had been a study of the casino issue and everyone had reached that place where the minds of all our people have come together as one mind."

When he says something like that, in his slow and gentle voice, it almost makes me cry. I wish our people followed the old ways more. And it makes me think of my dad. Before there was drinking, and the poverty and hopelessness that made Indians think drinking was a way back.

We continue on toward the center of the island. There's a little clearing in there where the trees don't grow, maybe because it is rocky and there isn't enough soil. Doda stops when we get to the edge of that clearing and motions down with his hand. I sit and he kneels down. We are behind one of the big spruce trees, looking into the clearing.

The cow moose comes out first. She looks around, moving her ears to hear in every direction. But we don't make any noise and the wind is not blowing to carry our scent her way. She walks across the clearing and two calves, ones that were born this spring, follow her. They aren't as alert as she is, so she watches out for them. A cow moose will fight a wolf, a bear, even a person, to protect her calves. Doda and I watch them until the cow moose walks into the woods on the other side of the clearing with the two calves behind her.

"I didn't know they were here," I whisper to Doda.

"They have come back," he says. His voice is soft but happy. For a long time there were no moose at all around here. They were all shot off a hundred years ago. It seemed like there would never again be moose at Penacook. But now they are back.

"All our old ones," Doda says, "they come back. Bear, beaver, moose, wolf, mountain lion," he says, listing all the animals that were killed off by the white hunters at the same time they were cutting down the forests and taking Penacook land. "They are all back now."

Doda lifts up his hands and looks at them. "Old hands," he says. "One day I get young ones again."

The way he says that scares me. I understand what he meant. "Doda," I say, "you're not going to die."

"You don't want to have to drag my body all the way back to the boat, grandson?" Doda chuckles. "No, not yet. I still got to use this body for some time yet."

Doda reaches out a hand and I pull him up to his feet. Doda looks at me with some surprise at how easy it was for me to do it. Like I said, I have been getting stronger. Then, slowly, he turns to walk back toward our boat. He doesn't say anything more until we get there. Then he looks around and takes a real deep breath before he speaks.

"Remember this, grandson," he says, "everything can come back. Just needs a place to come back to."

Like our island.

7 Taking Care

Something funny has been happening to me in school. I'm trying to understand it. I've always loved to read a lot, and I know I'm smart. But most of the teachers in the other schools I went to always seemed to assume I was a wise guy, a troublemaker. For some reason that isn't happening now.

At first I thought it couldn't last, but it is already mid-October and I'm still actually getting good grades. My best ones are in Language Arts, where I've been getting check-pluses on my homework.

Whenever there is a word that someone has difficulty with, Mr. Dougal asks the class if anyone can give him the dictionary definition. Nine times out of ten, I already know the word and I can see that he knows I know it. But he knows I won't be the first to volunteer the definition, and he lets other kids try to get it.

As I take my seat in homeroom this morning he nods to me. I nod back. I'm feeling more comfortable in school than I've ever felt before. Sometimes other kids even ask *me* questions about class.

There are still a few empty seats, and Mr. Dougal walks to the door to see if anyone else is coming in before he takes attendance.

Travis, the kid who sits next to me, leans over. "Chris, was it chapter five or chapter six we were supposed to read for Language Arts?"

Like Katie, Travis is in my homeroom and my Language Arts class. He's a skinny guy with reddish-brown hair and what must be the biggest collection of rock group T-shirts in the world. Every day he has a different one on. One day it is the Beatles, the next some grunge group from Seattle. Today Elvis is his guardian spirit.

"Chapter seven," I answer.

Travis groans softly. "I'm a dead man. No way I can read it before class."

It makes me laugh. "You'll do okay," I whisper, and then give him a quick summary of the chapter before Mr. Dougal starts roll call.

It isn't hard for me to talk to other kids anymore, even though I can't say I have a lot of friends. It is mostly still just Belly Button and Gartersnake and some of the other Penacook kids that I hang with. But not Pizza—Anthony. I don't think he's ever going to let anyone call him "Pizza" again now that he is a big football star.

Homeroom goes by fast. Now that I'm into things, it seems as if the school days have been getting shorter. The bell rings and we spill out into the hall.

As I walk down the hall toward gym, I see Pizza coming from the other direction. Maybe he sees me too, because he turns around and heads back the other way. Maybe he forgot something, but I don't think so. He is avoiding me and I've given up trying to talk to him.

Along with the other boys in my class, I go into the gym and head toward the boys' locker room. The gym isn't echoing with the sound of balls hitting the floor today. Instead, a long line of ropes that I haven't noticed before is hanging from the ceiling. They are about as thick as the wild grapevines that hang from the trees on our island. Each rope has a rubber mat under it. I hope it means we are going to climb them.

Suddenly, like fish at the approach of a shark, the guys around me scatter to the sides. A broad-shouldered figure is coming across the gym toward our group of sixth graders. They are giving him room to pass through like they can hear the theme from *Jaws*. But I just keep going. As we pass each other, he nods to me. I nod back. Ever since he talked to me in the downstairs boys' room I have had this kind of nodding acquaintance with Thumper Wheelock.

"You know Thumper Wheelock?" Travis says. I hadn't realized that he was behind me.

"Just to say hi," I answer.

"Just to say hi." Travis looks over at two of the other guys in our class, Brad and John. His voice sounds awed. "Just to say hi," he says again.

Coach Takahashi is waiting for us in the center of the floor when we come out of the locker room.

"Warm up first," he says.

Maybe it's the wood splitting and stacking that I have been doing with Doda that's made me so much stronger than I was a year ago. It's easy to do the push-ups and jumping jacks and the stretches. Before long there is sweat on my forehead and I feel almost the way I do after I've been sitting close to our woodstove.

Coach Takahashi isn't tall or even bulky the way Thumper Wheelock is, but every muscle is defined in his body. He was a champion wrestler in college and the kids say that he also has some kind of black belt. He isn't like the gym teacher I had last year, who spent most of his time yelling at the kids while he held a clipboard and watched. Coach Takahashi talks very softly and doesn't say much. Whenever he expects us to do something, he does it first himself. Not showing off, just demonstrating the right way.

"Today," Coach Takahashi says, "we're doing rope climbing."

He shows us how to hold the rope and use our legs.

"You can do it like this," he says. Then he climbs halfway up in less than the time it takes to count to ten slowly. He comes back down the same way, but a little slower.

"Don't slide down," he says. "It will burn your palms."

I rub my hands together as I wait.

"Just go as high as you want," Coach Takahashi says, "even if it is only a few feet. Be careful."

Finally, it is my turn. I grab hold and start to pull myself up hand over hand, forgetting about wrapping my legs around the rope. I've climbed like this before on the grapevines on our island, and even though the rope feels different than a grapevine, it feels familiar to me. The next thing I know, I am at the top of the rope and one of my hands is holding the support girder on the ceiling of the gym.

At first I don't hear anything, but then I can hear someone calling my name and people yelling.

"Chris, come down." It's Coach Takahashi.

I come down the rope the way he told us to. Controlled so that I don't burn my palms. I'm surprised to see that he is smiling. The other kids are looking at me in a way that I slowly realize is admiration.

"Where did you learn to climb like that?" Coach Takahashi says, a hint of laughter in his voice.

I shrug. "Grapevines."

"Grapevines." This time Coach Takahashi throws his head back and really does laugh. "Chris, we have to talk. With upper body strength like that—"

The bell rings and he doesn't finish his sentence. Instead, he just says, "Later."

I nod. I've never been praised before in school for doing something physical. I never looked for attention that way. But today was different.

As I head home that afternoon on our bus, I think about how different the bus ride must be now for Pizza. Though the farthest stop is Penacook, it isn't the only one. Not enough of us to justify a whole bus to ourselves. In the morning we're the first to be picked up, and for most of the trip we have the bus to ourselves. We sit where we want and we talk to each other. Then we hit what they call the outlying areas and other kids get on. Non-Indian kids. By that time we've all moved back a few seats and to the left side of the bus. No one has ever told us to do it. That's just what happens.

Or at least it used to happen that way before Pizza joined the football team. Now, in the mornings, Pizza stays in front, right behind Lou the driver, like he is navigating. Until the non-Indian kids get on, he mostly talks quietly to Lou, who likes Pizza. Lou is one of the few African Americans in Rangerville. He is a Vietnam veteran. He also works in the garage.

When the non-Indian kids get on, Pizza seems to wake up and come alive.

The boys who get on give Pizza high fives.

"Yo, Tony," they say.

Some of the girls smile at him. "Hello, Anthony."

And the distance between Pizza, and Belly Button and Gartersnake and me, just keeps getting bigger. When the bus is full, we aren't supposed to leave our seats or yell to each other. But the Penacook kids have their own sign language and we use it to communicate with each other. For example, a crooked index finger held up means "What's happening?"

Just this morning I crooked my finger and waved it to try to get Pizza's attention, but he wouldn't look my way. He won't look any of us from Penacook in the eye anymore. He sits all alone by himself in that front seat on the bus every morning.

He's not on the bus this afternoon, though. Because of football practice after school, he never takes the bus home anymore. He catches a ride with another kid on the team. Pizza seems happy, but seeing him changed this way is confusing to me. And what happened to me when I climbed that rope today hasn't made it any clearer. I liked the feeling that other kids were looking up to me. Pizza must like it too, but does that mean he has to dump all his old friends?

The wind that hits my face as I get off the bus is unusually cold, even for this time of the year. It is like the Moose Wind, the one that comes from the direction of the dawn, bringing the dangerous wet snowstorms they call northeasters.

Something is coming. I smell that something in the wind as I walk up the hill toward our house. And I hear a voice, a little voice calling my name in Indian. I look over to the side, half expecting to see a small person dressed in old-time clothing with a bow in his hand. Instead, I see a bird. It is late in the year for a meadowlark, but it is there and it is singing. That was what I heard calling my name, telling me to hurry.

I start running. By the time I reach the front of the house, Father Benet is coming out.

"Klis," he says, speaking my name in the old Penacook way.

Father Benet can speak Penacook pretty good. He knows that we have no letter "r" and that we always used to say "l" instead when we were given French and English names generations ago. He doesn't try to give sermons in Penacook, though. For one thing, there are quite a few people in the congregation who have never learned our language. Only about half the people at Penacook can speak it now. But also, he knows the story about the priest back a century ago who tried to give his sermons in Penacook and kept making mistakes. For example, if you try to say "Great Spirit" in Penacook and you pronounce one word a little wrong, you have said "Great Buttocks" instead. Every Penacook used to come from miles around just to hear that priest give his sermons.

"Klis," Father Benet says a second time.

It scares me when he does that, speaking my Christian name in Penacook the way Auntie sometimes does. For an awful moment I think maybe he has done that because it was the last word that Auntie spoke. That was why the meadowlark spoke to me and told me to hurry. Auntie was dying. And I am too late. She has died without me being here.

Father Benet can see some of what I am thinking. He holds up one hand, as if giving a benediction.

"It's all right," he says. "Auntie just forgot to take her medicine. Doda came to get me. I had her take her pills and her blood pressure went down. She is resting now. Doda is in there with her, making sure she gets some rest instead of getting up to make dinner."

Aside from the Indian health worker who comes twice a month to our clinic, there is no medical doctor at Penacook. When Father Benet came here many years ago, he came prepared to fill in not only as a spiritual helper but as an amateur medical one too. His house has as many medical volumes as it does books about Catholicism. Lately he's been reading a lot about natural vitamins and minerals. The joke is that now when he gives people the Eucharist he sometimes forgets and puts a vitamin C tablet on their tongues instead. But people trust him, and he is almost always the first one who is called when someone is sick.

"What pills?" I say, starting to go in.

Father Benet reaches down and puts his hand on my shoulder. It is a long reach. Father Benet played basketball when he was in college and he is about two feet taller than I am.

I look up at him.

"Christopher," he says, "Christopher. Your great-aunt has very high blood pressure. They haven't told you about that, have they?"

I shake my head.

"They don't want to worry you. I understand that. But, Christopher, just between you and me now, you have to look out for them. Just ask Auntie to remember to take her pill when you leave for school. And then ask her when you get home if she remembered to take the second one. You can do that, right?"

"Right," I say.

My voice is calm, but my heart is pounding. I feel

like a rabbit trying desperately to escape from a fox. High blood pressure. That was what she was talking about on the phone with Mito. She might die if she doesn't take her medicine.

Father Benet still has my shoulder in his hand. "Christopher," he says, "it's a big responsibility. It's hard to take care of people who are trying to take care of you. But I think you will find the right way to do it. You have a good heart."

Then he is walking down the hill, taking long strides. He is already halfway down the hill and I still haven't moved from the place I'm standing. But my heart isn't beating so fast now and I know what I have to do.

Take care of those who take care of you.

When I walk into the house, I call their names like always. But the answer doesn't come from the bedroom. I look over near the stove and see Auntie standing there, looking just as she always does. Her hands are covered with flour.

"Got a late start on supper," she says. "Celeste, she is playing over with her friends in Frogville. Maybe you can go get her in half an hour or so."

Doda, who is sitting in his rocking chair by the stove, nods at me when I look over at him.

It isn't easy to take care of those who take care of you. But I know that it is time to start trying. I walk over to the counter.

"First I'll help you make supper," I say.

I wait for Auntie to object, but she doesn't. I put an

arm around her and she leans against me for a moment. Neither one of us says anything for a while as the cuckoo clock on the wall that Mito bought her last Christmas keeps ticking and Doda rocks in time to the tick of the clock. Then she bumps me with her hip and pushes the colander full of potatoes and carrots over to me.

"Start peeling," she says.

I start peeling.

8 The Talking Stick

It's the last week of October and Katie still hasn't really said much of anything to me since the first day of school. Just the usual nods or hi's that kids give each other in the hall or before they sit down in class. I think maybe she is embarrassed by something I did or said. So I have been trying to apologize to her. But the harder I try, the harder I find it to actually say anything.

Weeks have gone by and I haven't been able to do it. Whenever there is a free moment and it looks like she is ready to hear what I have to say, my mouth doesn't seem to want to work. I've thought about writing to her instead. But whenever I have started to write notes to her I have torn them up before they are finished because they have all been terminally dumb. Unintelligible. Subanthropoid.

Today, though, as fate would have it, we have to talk to each other. We've been put into random working groups—or at least Mr. Dougal said he did it in a random way. My group has Katie and five other kids in it. We arrange our desks into one of four circles all around the room. Our task today is to choose the topic we are going to develop for a report. Then, over the next four weeks, we'll do research and put together an outline for a joint report, everyone writing a different section. Then we'll write the joint report and do an oral presentation to the class as a whole. That won't happen until after vacation break.

As we move our desks, Mr. Dougal writes these words on the board: CONTROVERSIAL. TOPICAL.

"This," he says, "is what your topic must be." He loudly taps the board with the chalk.

"But," Mr. Dougal cautions, "unrelated in any way, shape, or form to human reproductive activities, illegal intoxicants, or polyrhythmical musicality."

The kids who understood what he has just said giggle.

"No sex, drugs, or rock and roll," I interpret, surprising myself by speaking aloud.

"To put it bluntly," Mr. Dougal agrees.

Then everyone laughs.

"Are cigarettes okay?" asks a kid in the circle furthest from ours.

"To my mind," Mr. Dougal says, "they are an abomination. But as a topic, they're acceptable. Choose a group leader, and when you have made your choice, have your leader raise his or her hand. Remember, different topics for each group." He looks around the room to see if everyone is ready.

"Now." He raised one hand like a starting pistol, cocks his thumb, looks at his watch on his other wrist, and then lets his thumb fall as if shooting his imaginary gun. "Discuss!"

For a moment there is dead silence. Then, gradually, like a wave washing up on a beach, the sound builds as the kids in the room start to talk. In our group Katie is the first. She throws her hair back from her face and looks my way.

"I nominate Chris to be the group leader."

I'm stunned, but before I can say anything Travis speaks up.

"Yeah, let him be secretary and write it all down."

Katie shakes her head. "No, I'll do that," she says. "Chris for group leader, me for recording secretary. All in favor?" She raises up her right hand and says, "Aye."

Before I can say anything, everyone else in the group—except for me—has raised their hands and said "Aye."

For some reason I don't say no. Instead, I look around at the six kids who have just chosen me to lead them. I take a slow breath. I know that kids are all talking in the three groups around us, but in our group it is silent while the others wait for me to talk. I feel good. I'm smiling—and I never smile much in school.

"Okay," I say. "But we all have to agree to some rules. Okay?"

"What are the rules?" asks the red-haired girl

to my left. Melissa is her name. I look at her and each of the other kids, ticking off their names in my head. Melissa. Travis. Alicia. Brad. John. Katie. And me.

"Penacook rules," I say. "First is that when one person is talking, no one else can interrupt them. Okay?"

"Okay," they say.

"Second rule is that everyone has to agree with whatever we decide. If even one person doesn't agree, we can't come to a decision."

"Cool," Brad says. John, who is Brad's friend, pokes him in the ribs.

"Okay?" I ask.

Again everyone says "Okay."

"Kwey-kay," I say. Then I catch myself. "Okay, I mean. Now, to help us remember the first rule, we can use my pencil here as a talking stick. Whoever holds the talking stick is the one who has the right to talk. We'll pass it around the circle. Anyone who wants to talk can hold on to it. If you don't have anything to say, just pass it on to the next person."

"I like this," Brad says. John pokes him in the ribs again and everyone else in the group says "Sh."

"Okay," I say. "Let's start now."

I pass the stick to Melissa. She holds on to it for a minute and looks at it like she has never seen a pencil before.

"I just don't have anything to say right now," she

says. "But I want to hear what everyone else thinks."
Then she passes it to Travis.

Travis holds the pencil up as if were a microphone.
"I just want to say," he says, then he realizes what
he is doing and lowers the pencil from his mouth. "I
just want to say that I like doing it this way."

The talking stick pencil goes all the way around
the circle that way. Everyone is really serious about
it, as if we were sitting in a real council. Katie hands
the talking stick to me.

"Okay," I say, wondering what to do next. I look
over at the words on the board. "Now, um, this time
when we pass it around everyone can say what topic
they think we ought to discuss and Katie can record
it. Then the next go-around will be to comment on
everyone else's ideas."

I pass the stick to Melissa a second time. "I was
going to say abortion," she says, "but I think everybody is talking too much about it anyway and I
think it ought to be a private thing. So I don't have
any ideas right now, but I am really interested in
what the rest of the people in our circle think. I
really am."

Travis smiles as he takes the talking stick pencil.
"And I was going to suggest legalizing hemp. I saw a
thing on TV where you can makes clothes out of it
and use it for fuel and stuff. But I guess that is sort
of related to drugs, isn't it?" We nod, and now I'm
starting to get a little worried. Has Mr. Dougal's rule
cut off everyone else's ideas? But I know that at least

I have something I can introduce as a possible topic. I just hope it isn't the only one.

Alicia taps the talking stick pencil in the palm of her hand. "Fur," she says. "I think we should talk about how people shouldn't kill animals just to make fur coats." She holds the pencil out to Brad.

"Is rap music like rock and roll?" We all nod again. "Okay, I pass."

John, though, has an idea. "The V-chip," he says. "We can talk about that. It's such a lame idea."

Katie looks up at me as she holds the pencil, then puts her head down so that her hair flows across her face like a dark waterfall.

"Using Indian names for sports teams," she says.

It was the idea I had been saving to suggest. I'm so surprised that I almost fall out of my seat, but no one else seems to notice my reaction.

"Cool," Brad says. "Oops, I didn't say anything. You got the stick."

When Katie hands me the stick, I'm not sure at first what to say since her idea was the same as mine. So I admit it.

"I was going to suggest Indian names for sports teams too." Katie hands me the pad with the possible topics listed on it. I read them off. "Fur, V-chip, Indian names for sports teams. Does anyone have anything else they just thought of?" I look around the circle, ready to hand over the talking stick, but there are no other ideas. "So now we can start talking about them."

Once again the talking stick pencil starts to make its circle. This time everyone has something to say and it takes longer. By the time the stick has reached Katie both John and Alicia have decided they'd rather talk about Indian names than discuss their ideas.

We are all listening so close to what each person has to say that it is only when Katie gets the pencil and looks around that I notice what has happened in the room. All of the other groups have finished their discussions and are listening to ours. I raise my hand to show we have a topic, and Mr. Dougal nods and calls on each leader. He writes their decisions on the board.

Group One: SCHOOL UNIFORMS
Group Two: CIGARETTE ADVERTISING
Group Three: VIOLENCE IN TV AND MOVIES
Group Four:

Everyone is waiting for me to speak. I don't feel nervous. I won't just be talking for myself, but for our whole circle, and they'll be behind what I say.

I look over at Mr. Dougal. "Using Indian names for sports teams," I say.

Mr. Dougal nods his head again. "Thank you, Mr. Nicola," he says. "For your group's topic and for this lesson in participatory democracy. Now, desks!"

The room is filled with the squeaking sound of desks being moved, kids talking, books falling on the floor, the familiar chaos that disappeared so magically for a little while. Then the bell rings and we avalanche out into the hallway. But as we go, I catch the eyes of each of the people in our group—Melissa, Travis, Alicia, Brad, John, and Katie—and we grin at one another. We all know that the circle we made hasn't been broken.

9 Giving

According to Mito's phone call last night, he was scheduled to leave the center this morning. I've finished all of my Saturday chores. I've helped Doda and Auntie, keeping a close eye on her to make sure she doesn't overdo it with anything and that she has taken her medication. I've done my weekend homework and I've even put in an hour on our report about Indian names and sports teams. I'm trying to do as much research as I can on it, and the newspapers that Doda gets in the mail, *News from Indian Country* and *Akwesasne Notes*, have been a lot of help. I'm free now to do what I want with the rest of the day. I could go looking for Gartersnake and Belly Button, but I decide not to do that. I want to stay around home, just in case the phone rings. So I decide to take a ride instead.

I go outside, open the door of our old red Pontiac, and climb in. With one hand on the steering wheel I lean over, turn the key, and press the ignition button. Nothing happens. It has been ten years since there was a battery. But even if there was one, the old Pontiac doesn't have any tires and it sits up on blocks.

Doda and Auntie don't drive anymore. But I can imagine myself on journeys like the ones that Doda and Auntie used to take. This time of year, early November, they would be driving around New England, visiting their friends in other Indian communities, bringing food and special gifts. The backseat would be covered with boxes filled with Auntie's preserves, and in the trunk would be big fan-shaped leaves of dried Indian tobacco grown in Doda's special garden. That was the tobacco he would give away to his friends to use for their prayers, the way the old sacred tobacco is always used.

Auntie told me that they drove that circle of giving for forty-one years. They would go over to Maine to visit Pleasant Point and Indian Island, seeing their good old Passamaquoddy and Penobscot friends. Then they would swing down through Massachusetts to Gay Head and Mashpee visiting the Wampanoags. They would cut through Connecticut to see the Mohegans at Uncasville, cross over on the ferry to visit the Shinnecocks on Long Island, then go way up to the northern tip of New York State where the Akwesasne Mohawk Reservation is divided between Canada and the United States, before completing that big circle back at Penacook.

By the time they got back, Auntie had said when she told me about it, their car would be empty of the preserves and tobacco, but also full of the gifts that other people gave them. They would have driven so far, she said, that they should have worn out a set of tires. Then she giggled.

"But we never got a chance to wear out a set of tires," she said, explaining that one of their friends from Indian School who lived in northern New York owned his own garage. He always insisted not only on giving them a free tune-up each time they came, but on replacing anything that was worn out for free. "That Mike, he always gave us new ones."

The last of those trips took place before I was born. Just about all those friends that they went to the government Indian School with have passed on now. And the old car sits on concrete, not rubber. But I can feel their gifts when I sit in this car, surrounded by memory. Giving is so important to us Penacooks, to most Indian people, I guess. Doda told me how sorry he feels for wealthy people because they can only get that way by not giving as much as they should. The less you give, the poorer your spirit gets. The less you give, the less you are given.

Someone taps on the window on the passenger side.

"Can we come too?"

It is Celeste, holding her doll in the crook of her arm. I lean over and open the door, keeping one hand on the wheel so that I don't lose control. Celeste climbs in and places Buffy St. Mary carefully between us.

"Fasten your seat belts," I say, even though the Pontiac is so old that it never had any seat belts.

As Celeste pretends to fasten a seat belt around Buffy, she smiles at me.

"I know where we're going," she says. "We're going to pick up Daddy and bring him home to stay."

"Unh-hunh," I answer. It is all I trust myself to say because I suddenly have a big lump in my throat.

I start making engine noises and Celeste joins in with me. We do a pretty good job of imitating the sound of an old car as it roars across the countryside, heading for Boston.

Celeste is right. If this car could be driven, and if I was old enough to have a license, I would be driving it right now to pick up Mito. Celeste and I would be the ones to give him a ride home. It is early afternoon now, but he won't be here soon. It will take him the whole day to get here. First one Greyhound bus and then another, with lots of stops in every small town. Then he will have to wait for someone to get him at the last stop. By then it will be late at night.

Belly Button's parents are the ones who will pick him up there and bring him out to Penacook. They offered to drive the whole way to Boston and back, but Mito told them that he needed to make the trip by himself and they understood.

I hold the wheel so hard that it makes a creaking sound. I imagine what it would be like if I were driving my dad back here. I'd have the window open and one arm out. Celeste would be cuddled up right next to Mito, talking nonstop about all the things she was doing in school and about the stuff that she and

Buffy have been doing together. Then she would fall asleep, and my father and I would talk about things. He would ask about Doda and Auntie. He would tell me how they were going to be all right now that he was coming home.

(I would forget that his visit was only supposed to be a short one, just a trial visit to see how he does, fresh out of treatment. Or maybe in my version of things he would be cured, never going to drink again, ready to be home all the time with us. I would be tempted in my fantasy to have my mom be alive and well again, but I wouldn't go that far. Even in a fantasy I would know that was impossible.)

"*Wli,*" Mito would say in Penacook. "It is good." Then he would give me a compliment. He would tell me what a good driver I am now.

I almost say it is because I started to learn young. Mom used to let me sit on her lap when she was driving, and I would steer. I push that memory to the back of my mind so that my nervousness doesn't get the better of me, and I force my thoughts back to what I would do in my fantasy. In that world I would just shrug and say in Penacook, "*Wliwini, n'mitongwes.*" I thank you, my father.

Then we would talk about the plans to build the casino, and how we would stop it from being built on our island.

I take my hands off the wheel. Celeste looks over at me.

"Are we there yet?" she says.

I don't know what to say back to her. I'm just a kid who isn't old enough to drive. I am sitting in a car with no wheels. I don't know what we can do to stop the casino from happening, and I'm afraid that Mito won't know either. Why am I kidding myself? Nothing is going to get better. In one heartbeat I have gone from being optimistic and excited to being the world's biggest pessimist.

Celeste is still waiting.

Tap! Tap! Tap! Tap!

I look over and see Doda out there, tapping on the closed passenger's side window just the same way that Celeste did.

Celeste looks over at me and then looks back at Doda. Celeste is so much smarter than most little kids. She can tell that Doda wants to talk with me alone.

"Buffy and I have to get out here," she says. She picks up her doll, opens the door, and hops out.

"Want to give me a lift too?" Doda says, his hands on the old leather seat.

I don't know if I am in the mood to play along. But I nod and I say, without really intending to, "Okay, but I'm going a long way."

"I know you are," Doda says in Penacook as he gets in.

I put my hands back on the wheel. I don't really feel like pretending anymore, but I don't want to disappoint Doda. When grown-ups take the trouble to make themselves part of a kid's fantasies, the least a kid can do is pretend that he still believes in those fantasies himself.

Doda puts his hand on the dashboard, which is cracked with age.

"She used to be able to get up to eighty without even shimmying. Drove along just as smooth as glass," Doda says. "I hope one day you get a car that gives you as much pleasure as this one gave me. I think some day you will get such a car."

There is a funny tone in his voice. He is not just talking about the car. I take my hands off the wheel again and let them fall like dead birds to the seat on either side.

"Mito is not coming," I say in a flat voice.

Doda doesn't say anything for a while. He looks over at me. He knows that I am not the kind of kid who jumps up and runs away sobbing when he is disappointed. I am the kind of kid who just goes numb and sits unable to move. Doda looks me over carefully. At last he can see that I would not mind if he put a hand on my shoulder. In fact I want very much for him to put a hand on my shoulder. He does just that, and the warmth from his touch makes it possible for me to start breathing again.

"Why?" I whisper.

"He just called," Doda says. "He knows he is not ready yet."

"Why?" I say a second time.

Doda begins tapping his palm on the old dashboard softly, like he is playing a drum as he talks in a soft voice.

"He got up this morning. His overnight bag was all packed. But when he got into the bathroom and started combing his hair, he got scared. He got scared that he would not be able to keep himself from getting off the bus in one of those little towns and getting a beer. Just one beer to make the trip go faster. But it wouldn't just be one beer. And he wouldn't get back on the bus. And so he knew he wasn't ready yet."

Doda taps his palm on the dashboard one more time.

"His counselor told him that it took courage to admit he wasn't ready, to know that."

I don't ask when Mito will be ready. I know that Doda doesn't know. He keeps his hand on my shoulder. It rests there lightly, but it is like a jumper cable attached to a dead battery. It is all that keeps me going right now, all that keeps me from giving up. He knows what has just been taken away and he knows what he is giving me. I look over at Doda and I see the sadness in his eyes. He has had something taken away from him too. Part of my responsibility now, I see, is to give back to him. And to Auntie and to Celeste.

The dead birds that have fallen to my sides come back to life. They lift up to perch on the wheel and hold tight.

"Can't take my hands off the wheel when I'm driving," I say to Doda.

"Not when we still got such a long way to go," he says.

10 What Kind?

We're having lunch together, the seven people in our working group. Everyone has chipped in doing the research for our topic, and we've been sharing our ideas with each other. Brad came up with an article about a college that dropped its Indian mascot last year. We've got our outline written, and it seems like things are really coming together. Each of us will write our part of the report over Thanksgiving vacation.

It's the last day before the break. Starting the day we get back, the groups will have to present their "point of view," as Mr. Dougal calls it, to the class. Groups One and Two will go on Monday, and Groups Three and Four—that's us—on Tuesday. I'm beginning to feel worried about that in a different way. Maybe our presentation wouldn't be noticed in a really big school, but Rangerville Junior High isn't big. Some of the other kids in our group have been asked why we're so hot on criticizing the school name. This morning, when I walked down the hall, I saw a sign taped on the wall. CHIEFS FOREVER, it read.

But I have more to worry about than just that. Just

seven days after the school break the big meeting about the casino will take place at Penacook. The future of our island will be decided then. Thinking of that, I feel the familiar knot tightening in my stomach. It seems like the air is closing in around me, and it is hard to breathe.

While I am thinking about that, Brad looks across the table and asks me a question. I'm so deep in my thoughts, I don't hear it.

"What was that?" I ask.

"I said," Brad repeats, "what do Indians do on Turkey Day?"

Katie looks like she is about to say something.

"We do what we do every day," I say. "We give thanks."

"What do you mean?" Travis says.

"Thanksgiving is different for Indians," Katie says. I notice that her ears look redder as she speaks and I realize that she is actually angry. There was a time when I wouldn't have known what to say, but I've gotten to trust the kids in our group. So I tell them what I am really thinking.

"It's okay," I say. "It's kind of funny in a grim way. Think of what it's like for an Indian kid to go to a school where they're dressing the other kids up in phony Indian costumes with eagle feather headdresses made of paper and cardboard. You feel like they're making fun of your whole culture."

"I don't think people mean to make Indians feel bad about Thanksgiving," Melissa says.

"No, they don't. But that's the worst part. They

don't know that it hurts our feelings. They tell that story about landing on Plymouth Rock and starting their new colony. They don't mention why there was plenty of room for the Pilgrims to make their settlement there. English slavetraders brought smallpox to the Indians two years before the Pilgrims landed on the coast. When they got off the Mayflower the Pilgrims saw nothing but empty villages because all the Indians had died. And the Pilgrims themselves would have all starved if an Indian named Squanto hadn't helped them. And you know what? Squanto could speak English because he'd been taken as a slave to England years before that. And then when he found his way back to America, everyone in his village had died from smallpox."

I pause for breath. I've gotten into what can only be called a rant, but everyone at our table has been listening to me.

"Is that right?" Brad says.

"Yes, it is," Katie says. "And even after Squanto and the Wampanoags showed the Pilgrims how to survive, only a few years later the Pilgrims started making war on the Indians."

Travis whistles. "Man," he says, "that is hard."

"So do Indians hate us?" Alicia asks.

I look around the table at the concerned faces of the kids who have, I suddenly realize, become my friends. And all I can think of to answer them is a story that Doda told me.

"My grandfather told me a story. He said there

was this Penacook guy who lived next door to a white guy who hated Indians. One day the Penacook guy came home to find that his house had been burned down, his cornfield had been destroyed, and his dog had been shot. Whoever did it had left tracks and the Penacook guy followed the tracks right to the white guy's house. The white guy looked out the window and saw the Indian coming. That Indian looked mad! So the white guy ran for his life. But the Penacook guy was a great tracker. He followed him night and day, and the white guy couldn't get away. Finally, the Penacook cornered him.

" 'Are you the one who burned my house, destroyed my cornfield, and shot my dog?' the Indian asked.

"The white guy was quaking in his boots, but he managed to answer. 'I am,' he said.

" 'Well,' said the Indian, 'you better not let that happen again.' "

I look around the table. At first everyone looks stunned. Then Katie starts to laugh and everyone else joins in.

I start laughing too. As I laugh I think about how wise Doda is. He knows it isn't just what was done in the past that's important; it's also what we do now.

We talk a little more about things and finish off before the bell rings for the end of lunch. John and Travis move over to another table to talk with some friends who are on the hockey team with them. Brad gets up to go see if he can get another fruit cup from the lunch line.

Alicia looks over at Melissa.

"We have somewhere to go," she says.

"Where?" Melissa says.

Alicia kicks her. "Now," she says, and then tilts her head toward me and Katie. I don't quite understand what's going on, but I do notice Katie's ears have gotten red again. I wonder what she's angry about now. But she doesn't really look mad as the two girls get up and leave us alone, side by side at our end of the table, with five minutes to go before our next class.

Then I turn and look at Katie. She is fiddling around with her ballpoint pen. This the first time Katie and I have really been alone. We're in a lunchroom filled with kids, but more or less alone at this table. I take a deep breath.

"Can I ask you a question?" I say.

" 'Kay," she says. Her voice is softer than usual.

"What kind are you?" I ask.

Katie looks over at me as if I've asked her if she has just seen a flying saucer.

"Kind of what?" she asks.

"Of Indian, I mean."

Then she gets it. "Me?"

"Unh-hunh," I say. "Cherokee, right?"

This time her ears really get red and I can see that she *is* mad.

"Oh," she says, "you think I'm a Cherokee Princess, huh?"

There's nothing I can say, so I keep my mouth

shut. I find myself remembering what Doda said to me one day when Auntie got angry. When someone is quiet and gentle like Auntie and they don't get mad much, you'd better be quiet around that anger. I can still see the man she got angry at bursting out of our house like a partridge flying up out of a snowbank, Auntie's strong words at his heels. He had made the mistake of telling Auntie that they were ready to help her and Doda move into better housing and that they would be glad to arrange for their old shack to be demolished.

"You better run!" Auntie shouted. And that man ran so fast that his feet kicked up little spurts of snow. He ran down the hill and didn't stop until he got to the Tribal Development Office. I don't know what he told them, but there was no more talk about relocating Doda and Auntie. I wonder if I should start running now.

Katie stares at me, waiting for me to say something. I don't. She takes a quick breath. "Mohawk," she says.

"Mohawk," I repeat. I feel ashamed and stupid about thinking she was a Cherokee Princess.

"That's right. My father is from the Akwesasne Mohawk Reservation, the American side. Cook is a Mohawk name. And my real name is Kateri. I'm named after Kateri Tekakwitha, who's going to be a saint someday."

I nod. I know about the Blessed Kateri. It is kind of an irony, I suppose, that Penacooks know about a

Mohawk saint-to-be, seeing as how our nations were enemies only a couple of centuries ago.

"My mom's not Indian, but I live with her. My dad has been teaching me about being Mohawk. I don't see him a lot, but . . . ," Katie pauses. It is a very long pause.

"My dad's not around either," I say. "And my mom got killed in a car accident."

I feel dumb after I say it, like I am asking for sympathy. But I am still glad when Katie reaches out and touches the back of my hand where it rests between us on the table. Our eyes meet and then she pulls her hand back.

"I'm sorry about the way I asked if you were Cherokee," I stammer. "I feel really dumb."

"It's all right," she says. She starts putting away her notebook in her backpack as I reach out and pull my books toward me.

"Gotta go," she says.

"Me too," I say. "Bell's about to ring."

And it does and we go our different ways.

But I can still feel the touch of her hand on mine. And even though the Mohawks were our enemies for a while, I want to know more about them now. I want to know what Katie's dad has taught her about being Mohawk.

11 Adding Up

I am back, sitting by myself, in Doda and Auntie's old car. It's early in the morning, the Monday after Thanksgiving. I've gotten up before I usually do to watch the sunrise. The bus won't come for a while. This is the week we make our presentations in Language Arts. For some reason I'm not as nervous about that as I was. And for some reason I'm not feeling angry at Mito for not coming home like he promised he would.

I'm doing my mental arithmetic as I wait for the bus. But for once I'm not doing it because things are bad. My heart is pounding, but it isn't because I'm afraid. This time it's because things are going so well that it scares me even more.

Number One, I think. This is always my number one each day. I have made sure that Auntie took her pills. And I add to that thought that she has been looking stronger. And I hadn't even noticed before that she had been getting weak. Somehow, too, it has made Doda get stronger. Even though it is the

Freezing-Up Moon—"Creaky Joints Moon," Doda calls it sometimes—he hasn't acted as stiff in the mornings lately and he is smiling even more than usual when he looks at me. I'm not sure why.

Number Two. I have my dad's phone number at the Residential Center inside my pocket. In the letter that came Saturday he gave us that phone number and the hours of the day when they would allow him to receive a call. And his letter asked me to call him. I'm supposed to show the letter to the principal so that I can get permission to make a call from a school phone sometime this week.

Number Three. I am going to remember Laughing Louis. Even when things get bad, he still found something to laugh about.

Number Four good thing is Muskrat Mike and the song he played this morning on the radio: David Campbell's "Splinters of the Tree," which is this great song about how all the different Indian nations all over North and South America are part of the same great tree. That song always gives me chicken bumps on my arms when I hear it. It is about bringing us all together, healing the wounds between our nations and within ourselves.

As I walk to the bus stop, I add in Number Five. Number Five is, I have to admit, Katie. I am really looking forward to seeing her today. And for the first time I find myself thinking that we can keep on talking to each other even after we do our presentation. Aside from Celeste, Katie is the first girl I've ever thought of as a real friend. A good friend.

Number Six comes to me at the same time the bus crunches up, its tires in the gravel road making a sound like a giant's feet. I can see this Number Six in my mind, smell and hear and touch it all at the same time. It is the island.

I can feel the drum of my heart slow down and beat normally. It now has the even rhythm of a social dance song, not a jumpy, fancy dance beat. For the first time in a long time my mental arithmetic has all added up. Not one minus number. All pluses, or at least potential pluses. Too good to be true. But I think of Laughing Louis again and how his laughter always turned negative things around.

The bus door swings open.

"Hey-kwey, Lou," I say to the bus driver. I usually just nod to him, and it surprises him when I say that.

"Kwey-kay, Klis," he says back to me. I realize then how much Lou has been listening to us as he drives that bus, and I look at him differently. And we both smile.

I look up as Pizza gets on the bus. He's wearing a football jacket, like he always does now. As he comes up the stairs, he's looking toward the back and our eyes meet. I hold up my hand, but I don't do the usual Penacook sign language that we always used to do. Instead, I make a V with two fingers on one side and two on the other, like Spock does in *Star Trek*. "Live Long and Prosper."

I'm dead serious as I do it. Pizza tries to hold up his hand in the same way, but he can't get his fingers to spread apart just right. I take my other hand and pry my own fingers further apart, making the V bigger. Pizza shakes his head and makes this sputtering sound that passes for a laugh. We always used to kid him about that laugh that sounds like some kind of alien is stuck in his throat. He shakes his head again and then turns and sits down in the seat behind Lou. He doesn't come and sit with us like he used to do. But I can see that his shoulders aren't tensed up like he was a turtle trying to pull himself into a shell. He looks more relaxed now.

I put my hand on my pack. I've got my notes in there for our presentation. I'm all ready, even though our group won't go on until tomorrow. Number Seven is that presentation. But it isn't worrying me anymore. I'm looking forward to it now. I talked to Belly Button and Gartersnake about it over the weekend. They said, "Right on, Red Brother!"

Somehow, this morning, things are adding up for me.

Just before I reach the steps of the school I notice something on the lawn about ten feet to the side of the walk. I grab Belly Button's arm. He looks at me funny. I've grabbed him harder than I meant to. But I point with my chin toward the lawn. His eyes get round. The earth is soft there. They trucked in a lot of sand to make the lawns around the school, and grass has a hard time growing in certain spots. There, pressed deeply into the soil, are the large prints of a moose. Nobody else has seen them.

"Wli," Belly Button says.

"Unh-hunh," I agree, *"ktsi wli, nidoba."*

We can both see that moose coming in the night, standing there in front of the school, looking it over. Then turning and walking back into the woods that begin just the other side of the Rangerville athletic field.

In homeroom I find myself daydreaming about walking through the woods with that moose. In gym Coach Takahashi puts his hand on my shoulder.

"You okay, Chris?" he says. I realize that I have missed my turn and that he has just been calling my name. I didn't even hear his whistle.

"Sorry," I say.

"It's okay," he says. "I know about that report you and your friends are doing this week in Language Arts class."

I am no longer daydreaming now. My mouth is wide open and I am staring at him.

"About the team name and all that," he adds. He hands his whistle to the student teacher. "Phil," he says, "take over for a while." Then he hooks one finger and swings it toward the door. "Walk with me, Chris."

I'm in trouble, I think. Of all the people to have to explain our topic to, it would have to be the school football coach. If this were a few months ago, I would have been in tears by now.

As we walk, Coach Takahashi reaches out, without even looking, and pulls off a sign taped to the wall near the lockers. That sign, lettered in red marker, reads CHIEFS FOREVER, NO SURRENDER. I've seen other signs like it around school. I've been wondering who's been taking those signs down because they seem to disappear as soon as they go up. Now I know.

Coach Takahashi folds the sign and sticks it under his arm as we go into the office. He sits down behind his desk and I sit in the chair across from him. He places the folded sign on top of a pile of other similar signs. He notices me staring at them.

"You and the other kids in your class have stirred things up, Chris." Then he smiles. "Good for you."

I look at him. A coach is saying this?

"I just wanted to let you know that I'm behind you. I know that you aren't thinking of this as a movement. You're giving a report in class. But that is how you start to change people's minds. You make them understand your side and you present them with the facts."

I still don't say anything, but Coach Takahashi seems to read something in my eyes.

"Prejudice hurts," he says, "even when those who are prejudiced don't mean to hurt. And when you can get away with portraying people as less than human, demeaning them in words and images, you start to justify to yourself other ways to hurt them. Even worse ways." Coach Takahashi looks up to his right. I follow his gaze. There is a color print in an ornate gold frame of people who look like him, an older man and woman.

"My mother and father learned that. During World War Two, when the United States was at war with Japan, my father wanted to prove he was a real American. He enlisted in the army and fought as an American soldier in Europe. He was only one of many Japanese American men who did that. But his parents and my mother spent the war in an internment camp, Manzanar. They were American citizens, but because they were . . . 'Japs,' they were treated as if they were the enemy."

I still don't say anything. But that is okay. I know that Coach Takahashi doesn't expect me to say anything. He knows that I understand.

He looks at his watch. "There's one more thing I want to talk to you about, but we need to get back to class. Tell you what—bring in a note tomorrow saying it's all right and I'll give you a ride home from school."

"Okay," I say, wondering what he wants to tell me.

He scrapes his chair back on the hardwood floor and stands up. I do too. He reaches over and shakes my hand.

"Okay!" he says. "Back to gym class."

We walk down the hall together.

Language Arts is third period. As I go in and sit down I can hear some people whispering behind me, but the whispers end quickly when Mr. Dougal comes in.

We're Group Four, so that means we don't have to do anything today except listen. By the time the end of the period arrives, Group Two has finished right on schedule.

Before I go to lunch, where our group has agreed to gather for one last strategy session, I stop in at the office. I had dropped off the note about calling my father first thing when I got to school, and the secretary told me to check in at lunchtime to see about when I can make the call.

Mrs. Baxter, the school secretary, seems to be the person who works the hardest in the whole school. Everyone is always putting things on her desk. When I come into the office, she doesn't look up from the papers on her desk, so I stand there for a while until she notices me. When she lifts her head, she acts startled.

"I didn't even see you there," she says. "Now, you are here about your phone call?" She is flipping purposefully through a stack of notes on her desk. Her desk is never neat, but she seems to know where every single piece of paper on it is located. "Here," she says, "everything is arranged. You can come to the office and make your call at eleven forty-five tomorrow morning."

"Thank you."

As I enter the lunchroom, someone on the other side of the room does an imitation war whoop, "Woo-woo-woo-woo-woo," tapping their fingers across their mouth.

I don't know who it is and I don't look, even though I see a teacher heading in the direction the sound came from. I turn away to get in line and get my lunch, half expecting someone to trip me or jostle against me. But nothing happens. No surprises.

The surprise comes when I get to the table where we've agreed to meet. Two surprises. Katie is there, and John and Travis, Melissa and Alicia. But no Brad. That is a surprise because Brad had become so psyched about the project. Today he was supposed to bring in printouts from his dad's computer after doing a search on the Internet about similar situations where people were concerned about Indian names for sports teams and Indian mascots. The bigger surprise is that we're not alone at the table. Belly Button and Gartersnake are there, and so are all the other Penacook kids in school. Including Pizza. Who holds up a hand for a high five. I slap his palm.

"Kwey-kay, bro," he says.

"Kwey-kay," I answer.

"We're all here to give you moral support," Belly Button says. Gartersnake nods and raises up a fist to shoulder height to shake it in a Red Power salute.

As I look around at them and they all look at me, I am not quite sure what to say. Then someone squeezes in to sit down next to me. It's Brad. He slaps a pile of printouts onto the table. He's grinning like crazy, even though he has a bruise on the side of his face.

"Sorry I'm late," he says. "I ran into some hostile white natives. And I've got an idea."

"So do I," Katie and I say at the same time. We look at each other and then at Brad.

"You first," Brad says.

"My idea, actually my mom's idea," Katie says, "is that we should invite someone from the newspaper to class. School sports are such a big thing around here."

"Tell me about it," Brad says, touching the bruise on his face. "Anyhow, my dad thought we ought to invite in the school board."

I look at Brad and Katie and I can't help smiling. Their ideas are a lot like mine, which was to call the Penacook radio station and invite Muskrat Mike.

"That's great," I say. "Let's talk about it."

As we sit around the table and talk, Penacook kids and Rangerville kids alike, I feel our circle growing. Our minds, as Doda once said to me, have become one, and our thoughts are strong for the people. Before the lunch period ends, we're in agreement. We have to get the okay from the principal and Mr. Dougal, but if they grant permission, we are going to invite someone from the paper, the members of the school board, and Muskrat Mike.

The rest of the day is a blur to me. I hardly remember what happens in class because my mind is on the next day. We divide our duties up. Katie says she will talk to the principal, while I approach Mr. Dougal. They both consent to our plan. Then the other kids in our group each agree to contact a different school board member that night after school. Mr. Dougal has promised to call the newspaper and radio station.

At dinner I can hardly eat. Auntie and Doda talk some with me about the presentation.

"It is good that other people will be there, Klis," Doda says.

I tell them that I am set for my call to my dad tomorrow. Auntie smiles at that and then turns her head away to wipe her face as if she has just gotten something in her eye. I go to bed, thinking I will never be able to sleep, but the next thing I know I am opening my eyes and it is morning. Report Day!

12 The Report

Just before the beginning of the Language Arts class, people start coming into the room. Mr. Dougal raises an eyebrow as they all start to enter. He looks at me and mouths a couple of words: "Your guests."

The guests are the principal, the assistant principal, Coach Takahashi, and five older people I don't recognize right away. Two women and three men. Then I figure out who they are. I've seen their pictures in the *Gazette*. Four of them are members of the school board. The fifth one is the sports reporter for the *Gazette*. Then an Indian man slips in the door. I haven't seen him very often, but I recognize him. Muskrat Mike keeps a low profile at Penacook. Better to be heard and not seen is his motto.

"Hi," he says, "just finished my show. Hope I'm not late."

He has his long hair in braids wrapped with animal skin. He wears a cap that says BOSTON BRUINS in gold letters. Mr. Dougal nods at him.

"We're glad to have you visit our school," Mr. Dougal says. "I enjoy your show."

Katie, John and Travis, Melissa, Alicia, and Brad all look over as if they have complete confidence in me. I do not have complete confidence in me. I take out my notes and rearrange them. At least I try. But I can no longer read the words written on them, and I end up shuffling them like a deck of playing cards.

In front of the room Mr. Dougal is talking. His blurry mouth is opening and closing, but I cannot hear the sound coming out of it. There is a cloud all around me, thick as cotton. I feel like Gluskabe, the one the Creator made to prepare the earth for the human beings, before the Creator's lightning bolts struck and opened up his ears and eyes so that he could hear and see. This is the worst situation I have ever been in.

Then I think of Laughing Louis. What would he do in a situation like this? As I begin to smile, the cloud clears away from me. No lightning strikes, but I can see and hear. And, most of all, I remember that I can laugh and it seems as if I can hear Laughing Louis's voice telling me everything will be okay.

Mr. Dougal gestures to the seven chairs arranged in front of the class in a semicircle. "Since we have some special visitors today," he says, "I've decided to let Group Four go first. Group Four, please come up now to do your oral presentation."

I stand up on legs that feel as if they could jump over mountains. The others stand with me and we take our places. Except for Coach Takahashi, the grown-ups in the back are not smiling. But I smile at them.

"Before we start our presentation," I say, "I would like to tell a story that my uncle told me. A Penacook man drives into a gas station. The gas station attendant comes out and sees that the man is an Indian.

" 'Shall I fill it up, Chief?' the gas station attendant says.

" 'No,' the Penacook man says, 'just give me ten dollars worth, Mr. President.' "

Some people laugh, especially Coach Takahashi, attracting the attention of the Rangerville reporter, who is already making notes.

"The point is," I continue, "that every Indian man is not a chief, the same way that every non-Indian man is not the president of the United States. When you call someone by a name they haven't earned, it just becomes a joke."

Katie stands up. "Our topic today," she says, "is using Indian names for sports teams." She nods at Brad and Travis, who stand up to face each other.

"What team are you rooting for in the Super Bowl?" Brad says to Travis.

"I'm for the New Jersey Negroes," Travis says. "What about you?"

"I'm for the Jacksonville Jews."

Travis and Brad sit down.

"You see how strange that sounds?" Katie says. "But would it have sounded strange if they said they were for the Kansas City Chiefs or the Washington Redskins?"

The school board members in the back of the room

are looking uncomfortable. Or at least it seems that way to me. But the principal is whispering something to the assistant principal. Detention for Life, I hear Laughing Louis's voice say to me, and I smile.

We don't just make jokes to get our points across; we talk about history, about the real meanings of words such as *redskin* and *brave*, about the way American Indian people feel hurt and insulted when war whoops and tomahawk chops are done by crowds at sporting events. We use the information Brad got us from his Internet search, and we tell about the efforts being made by Native American activists, how schools all around the country have been changing the names of their sports teams so that they are no longer an insult to American Indian people.

No one has interrupted us, not even Mr. Dougal, who had held a stopwatch to time the other groups that did their point of view presentations yesterday. The stopwatch is facedown on his desk. And now I am standing again to make my final point.

"It has been said that giving a sports team an Indian name is meant to honor Indians. But if real Indians don't feel honored by that name, what really is the honorable thing to do?"

And that is the end of our presentation. I stand there and everyone looks at me in silence. In the back of the room Coach Takahashi gives us two thumbs up. Then he starts clapping.

The kids in the class begin applauding too, but the bell rings and the applause dies away. The guests start moving toward the doors. Muskrat Mike turns just before he goes out and gives me a little nod. Some of the adults are shaking hands with me and the other kids in our group. I look toward Mr. Dougal, who is standing near the blackboard by the list of the topics. He nods and then takes the chalk in his hand and writes a large check-plus next to Group Four.

A tall, stoop-shouldered man is shaking my hand. I don't know his name, but I think he is the school board president.

"Can't say I agree with everything you said, young man," he says, "but I would hate to be up against you in a debate. You have a career in politics."

As I put my things into my pack, our group makes a small, excited circle like a winning sports team. Brad holds out his hand and Alicia puts her hand on top of it, followed by Travis and Melissa and John and Katie and me.

"Wliwini," I say, "thanks, guys. We did it."

The hallways are empty as I walk down them toward the office. No mobs are waiting to tear me apart for impugning (calling into question, assailing by words or argument) the honor of our school. And there are no cheering crowds to congratulate me as if I were Rocky finally winning the heavyweight championship of the world. Everyone else is in their classrooms or at lunch. But I have my note in my hand and my call to make.

When I enter the office, Mrs. Baxter is waiting.

"I hear you just made quite a speech," she says. "Dr. Moody would like to see you."

I hold out my piece of paper and she shakes her head.

"Before you make your call," she says. She points her pencil toward the open door of the principal's office.

Dr. Moody is sitting behind his desk, reading something. The window is behind him and the light of the afternoon sun is shining off the top of his bald head. In his black suit he looks almost like one of those saints with a halo in the stained-glass windows at St. Anne's.

"Sit, Mr. Nicola," he says. His voice is slow and very deep.

I sit and he slowly lifts his head up to look at me.

"Was one of your relatives chief at Penacook some years back?"

"My grandfather," I say. I'm not sure I understand why he is asking me the question.

"Hmmm." His voice is like the rumbling sound of rolling boulders. He looks back down at the paper on his desk and taps it with his knuckles.

"We've had eighty years of . . . Chiefs at Rangerville schools." He looks back up at me. "And not one Penacook voice has been raised in complaint until now. Why is that so?"

I sit there, not saying anything. Dr. Moody is still waiting, and I realize that he wasn't asking a rhetorical question. He really wants an answer.

"Maybe they didn't think anyone would listen," I finally say.

He looks surprised. He opens his mouth, then closes it. "That *is* an interesting point," he says. He looks down at the paper on his desk and shakes his head. "That will be all, Mr. Nicola."

"Sir?"

"You can go now. I believe you have a telephone call to make."

When I walk out of Dr. Moody's office, Mrs. Baxter is waiting again. This time she smiles at me and her voice isn't so guarded.

"You can use my phone," she says. "I have to take something over to the high school." Then she leans close to my ear. "You did fine," she whispers. She goes into Dr. Moody's office and comes out with a piece of paper, the same one that was on his desk, in her hand. She closes his door behind her and says, "Take your time." Then she is gone.

The phone rings only once before being picked up on the other end. "Hello?" It is Mito's voice.

"N'mitongwes," I say. My father.

"Kinosis," he answers. Little boy. His voice sounds a little shaky.

Then we both quickly ask the same thing at the same time: "How are you?"

"I'm okay," our voices say together. And, realizing what we've done, we both laugh.

Mito clears his throat. I've heard him do that before when he has been crying. I listen close.

"I'm sorry I'm not there with you and Celeste, son. Can you forgive me?"

I could say that there is nothing to forgive. But Mito and I both know that isn't true.

"I can forgive you, Dad," I answer. My own eyes are full of tears and my voice is shaky. Neither of us says anything for a long time. I hold the phone close to my ear, listening to my father breathing, and I know he is doing the same, being touched by my breath.

Then we begin to talk again. He asks how everyone is doing. Doda, Auntie, Celeste. And I tell him how Doda is walking pretty good now, how I am making sure Auntie takes her medicine.

Then there is a silence between us. It isn't an uncomfortable silence, more like we are both thinking and our thoughts are together. Finally, it seems right for me to speak again.

"I've been thinking a lot about Laughing Louis," I say.

Silence again on the other end, and the sound of his breath. I wait. Then he clears his throat.

"Thank you, son," Mito says. "I need to think about Laughing Louis too."

After that I tell him about the presentation and he says he's real proud of me. Then he tells me about what it is like there in the center. He thinks he might be doing well, and I am certain that he's doing well. He's really, really trying this time, and I know how hard it is for him.

"Afraid I have to go now," he finally says.

We haven't talked about the casino. I'm not sure what to say anyway, but I'd been hoping that Mito would have an idea and that he would magically make everything right. But I've realized now that just trying to make *himself* right is taking all of his effort.

"Son?" he says, after I've been silent for a while.

"I'm still here, Mito."

"I can have another phone call this week."

There is a pad and a pencil on the desk and I write down the number again. If no one calls to tell us otherwise, we can phone him from home on Saturday afternoon. Then all of us, Doda, Auntie, Celeste, and me, can talk with Mito.

13 The Rest of the Day

After I finish my call, I start thinking again about what a day this has been. And it's only half over. I'm just a little worried now about how some of the older kids feel about me. I feel as if I've become a kind of lightning rod for the whole issue of the team name. And I still need to find out why the coach wants to talk to me.

As I sit there thinking, Dr. Moody comes out of his office and picks up an appointment book from Mrs. Baxter's desk. I quickly stand and say, "I'm all done." He nods and goes back to his office.

Now I can hear him talking on the phone with someone. I can tell from his answers what the conversation is about. His booming voice rumbles into the outer office like thunder.

"Yes, I'll be glad to be interviewed tomorrow about our team name by your crew from Channel Seven," Dr. Moody says. "Fine, I'll appear with the high school principal."

I am just passing the open door and he looks up as

he is listening to the person on the other end of the line. "No," he says to the person on the other end, "none of our students will be available for an interview." Then he actually smiles at me.

He starts talking again as I slip out the door and go to lunch. To my surprise no one treats me any differently than usual. When our group gets together in the cafeteria, I sit down next to Katie and we exchange grins. Then we all congratulate each other and talk about the presentation till the end of lunch period. But the rest of the day just goes by like any other. Finally, it is over and it's time to meet the coach.

As I walk out of the front door I see Thumper Wheelock standing at the bottom of the steps, his back to me. He turns around as the school door clanks shut behind me.

And he smiles. "Hey, heard you did a good job," he says. He holds up a hand as I walk down the steps, and I realize he wants me to slap a high five with him. I do it.

"I didn't put up any of those dumbass signs," he says. "It's okay with me if we change our name."

I don't know what to say, but Thumper's smile tells me that it doesn't matter if I am silent.

"So what do we call ourselves?" he says.

I almost say "human beings," but I bite my tongue. He's smiling, but he's serious. I look down at the ground and I see the moose print is still there. The whole school day has passed and its track is still there in the school lawn. Thumper looks where I'm looking.

"Hey!" he says, his voice both surprised and pleased. He kneels down and places his palm inside the huge footprint.

"Moose," I say. "That would be a good name for the team."

"Yeah," Thumper says. "I'd vote for that. The Rangerville Moose."

He thumps me on the chest. "See you later, Nicola." It is the first time he's used my name. I didn't know he knew it. But I nod. Then he winks at me and turns away.

Thumper swings down the walk and jumps into the car driven by an older girl whose face looks a lot like his. It must be his sister from the high school.

"Ready, Chris?" The voice comes from behind me. People aren't usually able to come up behind me without my knowing it. I turn around in surprise to see Coach Takahashi. His smile reminds me of Doda's.

I follow him to his car, a white Corvette with a baby seat in the back.

"That's for our daughter," he says. "I'll pick her up from day care later."

I put my pack in the backseat before I get in. I shut my door. He shuts his.

"Great car for a bachelor," he says. "But with another baby on the way we'll probably trade this in for a minivan." He looks over at me. "And I'm talking too much."

He starts the car, works the stick shift as smoothly as if he were a racecar driver, and we cruise out of the lot. Neither one of us is talking. Miles roll by.

Finally, Coach Takahashi clears his throat. "It's really two things I wanted to say to you, Chris. First is I need to thank you. I've been at Rangerville for three years. May seem long to you, but it's not to a coach. A new coach. Chris, I don't like prejudice. I don't like racial stereotyping. But I hesitated about bringing up the issue of the name. I wasn't sure that I was the one to start talking about the implicit racism in the way they've been using Indians as icons." He looks over at me to see if I'm following him.

I nod.

"And now that you've called so much attention to it, Chris, I'll back you up. It won't be easy."

"That's okay," I say. "It's never been easy." I think about my mother and Mito, about Auntie's blood pressure and the pain in Doda's legs, about the island and how we have to find some way to save it. I'm silent longer than I intend to be.

Coach Takahashi looks over at me and nods. "No," he says, "I guess it hasn't been easy for you, has it? Anyhow, thanks. Thank you, Chris." He taps the wheel with the knuckles of his left hand and then takes the curve that leads down into Penacook.

"Second thing," he says. "How much do you weigh?"

"A hundred and twelve pounds."

"Perfect. I had this idea . . . well, actually it

wasn't just me. It was Dennis Wheelock. He says he knows you."

"Thumper?"

"Thumper. You know I'm the coach of the wrestling team. Thumper is my heavyweight. Probably team captain this year. He thought you'd make a good wrestler. Want to give it a try? Join the team?"

I take a deep breath and then I hear someone saying "Okay." And since there are only two of us in the car, and Coach Takahashi was the one waiting for an answer, I realize it must have been me. I smile as I say it again. "Okay. I'll give it a try."

I can see from the look on Coach Takahashi's face that even though he has been at Rangerville for three years, he has never been out to Penacook before today. But there are plenty of people who have lived their whole lives in Rangerville without ever coming within two miles of our little reservation, so he is doing better than most. Almost the first sight that greets us when we turn onto the reservation road is the blackened ruin of the big house. That burned-out house and the huge overgrown yards around it are on the very edge of our rez, the closest Penacook property to the state road. No one has ever built there, in part because Mito has never allowed anyone else in the tribe to use the land, in part because no one has ever wanted to use it.

Half a mile further down the reservation road we come into the main part of town. The fading light makes the trailers and the small, worn-looking houses look even worse than they do in midday. And this time of year is also sort of grim. No leaves on the trees and no flowers to cover up the patched roofs, mismatched shingles, piles of firewood, stacks of salvaged used lumber, car bodies, and old pieces of machinery and other useful junk that accumulates around most people's places. Here and there is an occasional brand-new trailer with an attempt at a lawn in front of it, and there is the new modular office building that is the tribal headquarters with the split-level log cabin up the hill behind it that is the chief's home.

As we cruise past the tribal office, I can see our police chief watching us from inside the patrol car parked out front. Not making it obvious, but keeping an eye on this new strange car that has just pulled onto the rez. We all have this kind of Indian radar that picks up whenever someone strange comes onto the rez. I know as we drive along the road that every house has at least one set of eyes looking out to watch us go past. Uncle Buster sits in the passenger seat of the car while his deputy, Sam, stands outside leaning against the driver's door. Sam has his coat off and is flexing his muscles, his thumbs hooked in his belt while he looks down at the ground. I roll down my window and wave a hand at them. Sam just keeps flexing his muscles, but Uncle Buster waves.

"Which way, Chris?" Coach Takahashi asks. It

seems to me that he has been trying to be quiet ever since passing the ghost house. I appreciate that. I can imagine how someone else might show how shocked they are at how poor our community is in a sympathetic voice that makes you feel small enough to sit on a dime and still swing your legs.

"Over there," I say.

"That's a church."

"Unh-hunh."

"You live there?"

"No, I see Father Benet. Want to meet him?"

Father Benet is towering at the top of the church steps as we pull up. It seems as if he has absorbed some of that Penacook radar that we all have. He walks down the steps with a smile on his face.

"Father Benet. And you must be Coach Takahashi," he adds before I can say anything. He reaches down to grab Coach Takahashi's hand in a firm grasp. "Good of Chris to bring you here. I'm glad to meet you. Our boys think highly of you. Anthony, in particular. You've helped that young man find a new sense of pride. It hasn't been easy for him."

"Pleased to meet you, Father."

Then they start talking as if they have known each other for years. I'm not saying anything, but they both keep looking at me as they speak, including me in their conversation, and I don't feel left out. I nod every now and then and that is enough. As they talk, I'm surprised to find out how much Father Benet knows about what goes on at the Rangerville middle school, including the controversy about Indian team names.

"You must be proud of Chris here," Coach Takahashi says.

Father Benet looks at me. He knows praise like that is embarrassing to me, but the look in his eyes seems to be saying that I should accept it.

"Christopher," Father Benet says slowly, "has the heart of a chief."

When their conversation ends, I tell Coach Takahashi that I don't need a ride the rest of the way up the hill to my house. There are some things I have to talk about with Father Benet.

"Maybe next time," the coach says. And he means it. I can tell that although this was his first visit to Penacook, it won't be his last.

As he drives off, I wave at him until his car vanishes over the hill. Then I smile as I watch Sam get into the tribal patrol car across the street. Keeping a respectful distance, he and Uncle Buster follow Coach Takahashi to escort him safely off Penacook land. And, I think, to give him a tribal speeding ticket if he goes too fast before he leaves the reservation road.

14 Looking for the Pony

On Saturday morning I walk down to the edge of the lake. It may be the Freezing-Up Moon, but the waters of the lake are not yet covered with ice. I've brought the oars down with me. I push the boat out and jump in. Then I row slowly out toward the island, the creaking of the oarlocks almost like the rhythm of an old song. So much has been happening that I need time to think.

I pull the boat up on the shore and walk back among the trees to sit on the trunk of a fallen cedar tree that is sheltered from the wind. I pull my cap down tighter around my ears, button the top button of my coat, and pull my knees in close to my body. The early December sun is shining down on me, and I don't feel cold, even though I can see my breath. Alone at last, I start to add up the events of the week.

The day after our report a story about it appeared on page 3 of the *Gazette*. Aside from the corny headline, "Too Many Chiefs," it made our report sound good. "A number of special guests, including this reporter, were invited to attend this classroom discussion. The students earned unanimous praise for tackling a sensitive issue with humor and intelligence." It quoted Principal Moody—"gave us all food for thought"—and "Local Native American Radio Personality" Michael Muskwas: "Among our people the word 'Chief' was always used to honor our leaders. Calling an athlete 'Chief' would be like calling a movie actor 'Pope.' "

It also quoted Coach Takahashi, who said that "after a meeting with student athletes from both the junior high and the high school, real interest in exploring a new name for the Rangerville teams was expressed." The next day there was an editorial praising the idea of a new team name and a letter from the head of the school board. And on Friday the newspaper announced a contest for a new name. Katie and the rest of our group are going to vote for "the Rangerville Moose," and with Thumper's support I bet we can get lots of other kids to vote for that name too. The Coalition will help us, I'm sure of it, and that includes Pizza.

As I think about it all, I feel good. What I've done and said has been listened to. It has made a difference. If I'd just given up and not tried to do anything, none of this would have happened.

There is this story that Doda loves to tell. It seems there are two brothers. One of them is always happy and one is always grumpy. Their father is worried about them, and so he goes to a wise medicine man for help.

"What can I do?" the father says. "It isn't right for one brother to always be happy, no matter what, and for the other one to always be pessimistic."

"This is what you have to do," the medicine man says. "Take two lodges. Fill one with good things to eat and things to play with. Then put Grumpy into that lodge and leave him there all day. At the end of the day open the door and see how he feels then. Fill the second lodge with horse manure. Put Happy in there and leave him there all day. At the end of the day open the door and see how he feels then too."

The father liked that idea and he built those two lodges. He filled one with good things and put Grumpy inside. "Stay here until I come for you," he said. Then he shut the lodge door. He filled the second lodge with horse manure and put Happy inside and told him the same thing.

At the end of the day he opened the door of the first lodge. All the food had been eaten, all the toys had been broken, and Grumpy was sitting on the floor with a scowl on his face.

"I'm bored," Grumpy said. "There's nothing to do in here."

Then the father opened the door of the second lodge. To his surprise he saw Happy digging in the horse manure, a big smile on his face.

"What are you doing?" the father said.

"With all this horse manure," Happy answered, "there's got to be a pony around here somewhere!"

So much depends on the way you look at things. That is what Doda is always telling me, and I see how right he is. Instead of giving up, I have to look for the pony.

A birch leaf flutters down from one of the tall trees and touches my cheek before it strikes the ground. Every leaf that falls returns to the earth and helps feed the roots of the trees. Then they grow more leaves. That is the natural cycle. We've been learning about that in our science classes ever since I can remember, but I suddenly find myself thinking about it in another way.

Everything has to be part of that cycle, which is just like our old Penacook idea of the sacred circle of life. If things don't remain in that circle, they don't stay in balance. And a picture that has been in my mind for days comes into focus. It is the ghost house at the edge of the reservation. A house and land that no one will use. Kept out of the cycle, even though it is near the main highway. But if it was to be used in the right way, it could save our island.

I pick up that leaf and look at it. "Thank you," I say to it. Then I walk down to the boat and row back to the mainland. I need to talk to Doda and Auntie before our phone call to Mito this afternoon.

15 The Council

When I open my eyes, I can't believe it is morning. The sun slanting through the white curlicues and fern leaves that the Frost Spirit painted on the window makes patterns on the wall next to my bed. I thought I was too excited to sleep, especially after the way Auntie and Doda and Father Benet and I talked until late in the night about what would happen tomorrow at the Tribal Council meeting.

But tomorrow is today, Sunday. I look at the clock. It is still too early for the chief to have gotten back from Boston, his briefcase full of papers and proposals. He hasn't been back to Penacook for over a week. Talking with the backers, those people who will put up the money to build the casino, provide the gaming machines and the other furnishings, and then take a share of the profits.

"The same share as the Mohegans are giving their backers," the chief said at the last meeting. "A good deal for us."

Although he is a reborn businessman, talking about

it the way some people talk about religion, people here don't think that our chief is crooked. He really does want to make money so that the lives of our people can be better. He grew up here in one of the most run-down houses on the rez and then went out to make money working construction, saving most of what he earned. He tore down the house and built his new split-level log cabin on the same site, and his mother lived in that log cabin, proud of her son, until she passed away a year ago. But our chief also seems to have forgotten that there are some things we can't sacrifice for money.

That is what Doda says. "But tomorrow," Doda said last night, "we may remind him of some things."

I turn on the radio, just in time to hear the last few words Muskrat Mike speaks before the next song.

"So everyone make it to today's council meeting. Keep those generations to come in your heart along with the land that we're taking care of for them," Muskrat Mike says. "I'll be there with bells on."

He shakes something that has the kind of bells that powwow dancers wear. Then Floyd Westerman's deep, throaty voice is singing "La tierra es su madre." The earth is your mother.

The day goes more slowly than any day I can remember. After Mass I help Doda stack wood, but he keeps being interrupted by people who come to see him. They are all talking about the same thing. I lose count after the twentieth visitor.

Celeste is walking around with Buffy and singing. After talking with Mito and telling him my idea, we put Celeste on the phone with him. She's been singing almost nonstop since then. She looks over at me and stops singing for a minute.

"Buffy is so excited," Celeste says, "that she just can't stop singing."

After dinner Father Benet picks us up in his truck to drive us down the hill to the meeting. He has a folder on the seat beside him and he hands it to Doda as we get in.

"Fresh off the church fax machine," Father Benet says as Doda looks at the contents of the folder, nods, and then hands it to me. I read the two pages of my father's message carefully as we roll slowly down the hill.

There are cars parked all around the tribal complex, some of them from out of state. Tribal members coming home for the big meeting. There are hardly any seats and I wonder where we will sit until someone comes up to us. It is Muskrat Mike.

"Saved the best seats in the front for you folks." He pokes me in the side with one long skinny finger. "Right on, Little Warrior," he says.

When our chief takes his seat you can see that he knows something is up. You can also see that he has only heard rumors about what it is. He looks a little confused. The meeting is called to order and the minutes are read. Old business. Everyone is waiting, I can tell.

Doda stands up. "I have been asked by my son to share this letter from him," he says. Then he says something in Penacook that means "For the people, for the children, for the earth." He says it so fast that the chief, who has forgotten a lot of our language, doesn't catch it.

"What was that?" says our chief.

"Point of order," says Doda. Everyone laughs. It is one of the chief's own favorite sayings, straight out of *Robert's Rules of Order*, the official handbook for running a meeting.

"Is this pertaining to the site of the casino?" says our chief.

"Per-tain-ing," Doda says, drawing out the word. Everyone laughs again.

"Go ahead," our chief says. There's nothing else he can say.

Doda looks over at me and motions for me to stand up. "I would like my grandson to stand beside me and read this letter from his father. My eyes are not so good anymore."

I take the letter from Doda's hand and I stand next to him.

" 'My friends, my brothers and sisters, my people,' " I read, " 'you know who I am and you know my family. It is a family that has always stood strong for our Penacook people and for our sacred land. You know, too, how often I have let you all down. Even though you are all in my heart, I have let alcohol weaken my spirit and I have not worked for you or cared for my family. Now I am trying to change that and to make amends to those I have injured, even though I know that I do not deserve your forgiveness. So I have written this letter, a letter that will be followed by a notarized document.' "

I pause and look up from the letter. It's so quiet in the building that I can hear Auntie's breathing from the seat just in front of me, even though it is hard just now for me to see anything because my eyes are getting blurry. I wipe my eyes with my sleeve to clear them.

" 'The issue of the casino has divided our people. The proposal to build that casino on a place in the heart of our land has been like a decision to cut out the heart of our people. But I can see that our people need the income from a casino to help them survive, to give them the pride of being able to support themselves and their children.

" 'Our family has always defended the heart of our land. We will not stop doing that. We will never allow a casino on our island. I will come and stand in front of the machines and my blood will flow from my body before I will allow that to happen. I promise you this as the son of a chief who was himself the son of many chiefs before him.' "

Some people are moving in their seats now and I can tell that Mito's words have made them nervous. But I don't stop reading. I go on quickly to the next page.

" 'But no blood should flow on our sacred land. If

we have to sacrifice a part of our land, it should not be the heart. With this letter, my family and I give to our people a place where a casino can be built. It is the property I own at the edge of our reservation, a place close to the roads that will bring people here. And, seeing good come to our people, the spirits of my family will be soothed. Those who died by fire in that place, their spirits will be quiet and will bless our people. We give you that land. Build your casino there.' "

Doda's hand is on my shoulder as I keep standing. Celeste is standing next to me on the other side with her arm around my waist. I look down at Auntie and see that she is smiling and crying. I can hear the voices of the people in the room. They are calling for a vote on my father's proposal.

"We will need to study this," our chief is saying.

But his voice is weak compared to the voices of our people in that room, voices joined together in a circle of agreement.

"We have a second on the proposal," Uncle Buster calls out.

"Is there any discussion?" says the chief. He looks around the room.

"Call the question," says Muskrat Mike.

The tribal secretary reads it aloud. "Be it resolved that the first choice for the siting of the tribal casino will be the Paul Nicola property at the western edge of the reservation boundary line. All in favor signify by saying Aye."

The "Aye" that comes back is so loud and so strong that it shakes the building like a giant roar of thunder.

"Those opposed?"

There is silence. Even our chief, who seems to be realizing that what has happened is not only the will of our people but also the best idea, says nothing.

"The resolution is passed."

People are shaking Doda's and Auntie's hands. They are smiling at me and shaking my hand too. I hear their words of praise and I thank them. And I know that whatever happens to me from now on, whether it is good or bad, I will always remember this: that the heart of a true chief beats with the hearts of the people.